VOWS & VENGEANCE, CONFESSIONS OF A CLOSET MEDIUM, BOOK 4

NYX HALLIWELL

Beach Path Publishing LLC

Vows & Vengeance, Confessions of a Closet Medium, Book 4

© 2021 Nyx Halliwell

ISBN: 978-1-948686-45-7

Print ISBN: 978-1-948686-46-4

Cover Art by EDH Graphics

Formatting by Beach Path Publishing, LLC

Editing by Beth Neal, Patricia Essex

Please Note

❦ 1 ❦

"We want to renew our vows," Mama says, "at the anniversary party."

She sits on the edge of the chair across from me in my office, Daddy beside her. Both grin from ear to ear.

"That's awesome." I hide my concern about the celebration being only five days away. Their thirtieth wedding anniversary is a big deal in and of itself, and I'm thrilled at the idea. I'm just not sure how to add a vow renewal on top of the rest on such short notice. "What brought this on?"

Dipping her chin, she reaches over and takes Daddy's hand, intertwining their fingers. I swear she bats her lashes at him. "Do we need a reason? We've been through a lot in our married life, and well, it feels right."

"Okay." I drag over my paper planner and flip to Saturday's page. It's already filled with a dozen to-dos, sticky notes, and highlights. "I'll see if Reverend Stout is available to perform it."

"Oh, we don't want him, Ava." Her tone suggests I'm being silly.

I glance up. "Why not?"

Her eyes, so much like my own, appear a bit surprised. She

sighs dramatically and shoots Daddy an exaggerated look. "You're an officiant. Why wouldn't we have you do it?"

"Me?" While it's true I can conduct ceremonies, my experience playing minister is limited. Since taking over my Aunt Willa's event planning service, I've only married one couple in the gardens behind the house. It's part of my modest bridal package for those who prefer a small-scale affair with fewer than twenty guests.

In Thornhollow, Georgia, bigger is always better when it comes to social gatherings, as evidenced by my parents' upcoming celebration with an expected attendance of nearly four hundred. "Mama, I'll have my hands full running the party. Surely, it would be better to have Reverend Stout do the honors."

"What more do you have to do?" She seems truly perplexed at my resistance. "All our friends and family are already invited, Betty Lee has the flowers ordered, Queenie's preparing the food, and Brax and Rhys are taking care of the decorating. The hotel is perfectly equipped with a bar and anything else we'll need. Don't you see? It's perfect."

She's correct, but I've learned that on game day, things often don't go as well as they should. Caterers and florists are like the rest of us—they get sick or their car breaks down. A location such as the hotel suddenly has a flooding issue, or a storm washes out the road to it. Since I moved home last fall, I've had both occur. Just two weeks ago, one of the elderly guests at a wedding passed out thirty seconds before the bride was due to walk down the aisle. Luckily, the woman was simply dehydrated, and after the ambulance whisked her off to the clinic to be checked, we resumed. But stuff happens.

However, seeing the way Mama keeps glancing at Daddy like a dewy-eyed school girl, how can I say no? Not even my dislike of speaking in front of large groups would make me disappoint her if I could keep from it. "All I want is for you to be happy, so if you want me to officiate, I'd be honored to."

Mama always gets her way, regardless of the circumstances.

Seeing the expression of delight on her face at my acquiescence is worth the unnerved cramping in my stomach. She claps once and digs in her purse. "Excellent. Your father and I have some ideas for the script."

Great. Hopefully that makes my job easier, but when is life with my mother ever easy?

I accept the paper she hands me and glance over the itinerary. Being mayor of Thornhollow, she's exceptionally detail-oriented and organized. The agenda in front of me is nothing short of a full-blown ceremony, complete with several musical numbers. My dad is a musician, so no surprise there, and the one saving grace I see is that the two of them plan to write their own vows. All I need to do is conduct the opening, and then close the ceremony.

"We'd like you to add your own words about our family and what it means to you before we recite our oaths to each other," Daddy says, killing my hopes of getting off light.

"Of course." I smile. "Looks like it's going to be a beautiful event."

"You're going to compose your own vows, right?" Daddy teases Mama.

She playfully boxes his arm. "Of course, I am."

"Why wouldn't she?" I ask.

He winks at me. "She has Candace writing her speeches now. Just making sure she isn't writing the vows too."

Candace is her newest executive assistant. A dramatic eye roll accompanies feigned exasperation. "You are incorrigible. I only have her tweaking my words. She's young and has a way with the eighteen to thirty-year-old demographic."

Her phone rings and she fishes it out. "Speak of the devil, I have to take this. I'm sure she's anxious about where I am."

She hops up from the chair and paces from my office at the front of the house. Daddy sits forward, watching her. "This means the world to her," he says in a hushed tone. "You need to do everything you can to make the day special."

I don't miss the fact that he excluded himself in the statement. "I am honored that you want me to perform the ceremony."

He raises an eyebrow. "But...?"

"No buts. You know I hate speaking in front of people, that's all. The two of you are good at it—having the spotlight on you. Me, not so much. I do my best work behind the scenes."

"What are you going to do when you marry that Cross fellow and his mother invites the entire county, plus, all their relatives from up north?" He winks at me. "Better get used to being in the spotlight, baby girl. You were born for it."

I chuckle nervously and glance at the gorgeous diamond on my ring finger. "I was so *not* born for it, but thank you for reminding me to panic about my own upcoming wedding. If, that is, Logan ever gets a break from the Gullen case, and Mrs. DeHavilland's divorce gets pushed through before Hades freezes over."

On Valentine's Day, the love of my life proposed and I said yes. I've dreamed of having it in June, but that's only a month away and we can't make solid plans, due to Logan's current caseload. As the only attorney in town, he's up to his neck with a lawsuit against the owner of the old metal works property and a divorce that's making the news every night. As it stands, he has to be in court every day for the next six weeks, and that means we can't throw the bash his mother is demanding until fall. I'm disappointed, but my own business is expanding, too. Delaying our wedding so we can enjoy our ceremony, rather than feeling stressed out by it, seems wise.

"You'll be walking down that aisle before you know it," Daddy says, standing and stretching. "And I'll be one proud father escorting you."

Mama rushes back in, shoving her phone away and grabbing her purse. "Gotta run. WRTV Channel 5 wants to do an interview about Founder's Day." She kisses Daddy and hustles for the door. "Don't forget, one p.m., Ava. Get there early if you can. I want a photo of you and Amos Butterfield. It will make a great promo shot for the Chamber."

"Who?" I ask.

She looks at me flummoxed. "Amos 'Mastermind' Butterfield? He's the state historian, and the bestselling author of the Murder in the Heart series. Honestly, Ava, didn't you read the info I sent to everyone on the committee?"

Stepping into my aunt's shoes, I inherited her position as president of the Chamber of Commerce. Usually, I let the VP, Baylor Davis, take care of things and she does a great job. She's the town's librarian and is as organized as Mama. Occasionally, however, I can't get out of at least pretending to run the volunteer organization. Vaguely, I remember scanning the email, but I didn't open the attachment. "Sorry. My mind has been filled with other goings-on."

"Well, he's quite famous, and he's looking at significant historical places in our state for the setting of his next murder mystery." She claps. "Being in one of his bestselling stories could catapult our little town to stardom!"

While that would be a feather in her cap, I'm not sure some of the townsfolk would be as excited about it. The tourism would certainly get a boost, though, and that would help everyone. "I'll be there with bells on."

"You better, and wear something appropriate." As I glance down at my black pants and purple top, she turns to Daddy. "You'll be there, right, Nash?"

"Honey, a horde of zombies couldn't keep me from it." He opens the door for her. "Good luck with your interview."

She waves at us and Rosie, my office manager, calls, "Goodbye, Miss Dixie," from her office across the way.

"Bye, Rosie. Kiss Fern for me." In a flourish of Chanel No. 5 and the swish of linen, she's out the door and down the steps.

"Your mother is a force of nature," Daddy says, a gleam in his eye. He watches her hustle down the sidewalk in her signature dress suit. The spring wreath Rosie hung on the gate nearly falls when Mama slams it too hard in her haste. She's texting someone as she gets in her car. "I've never met anyone like her."

"About your vows." I glance across the street to Logan's place. I see his car is out front and I think about skipping the Founder's Day thing and sneaking over to see him. Mama would kill me. Twice. "Do you need help writing them?"

He squeezes my shoulder. "Nope. Got 'em done already."

There's a twinkle in his eye that reminds me of my youth when he always had something fun up his sleeve. "Good for you."

"Don't tell, it's our secret, but I'm going to sing them to her."

Daddy and his guitar. I smile. A former cop, he left that life behind and pursued his dream of forming a band. They're no longer together, but he's semi-famous anyway. Although he's cut back on his live performances so he can stay in town, he's started his own YouTube channel and posts new songs, as well as a few oldies, every week. His following is close to twelve thousand and growing.

"That's awesome. She'll love it." As will all his fans, because, dollars to donuts, someone in the crowd will record the whole thing and post it before the ceremony is even finished. "Mama need look no further than her own backyard for a famous guy to *catapult us to stardom*." I use my best imitation of her voice.

He laughs. "I don't know about that. Sounds like this Butterfinger guy is the real deal."

I don't correct his error on the name. "No matter, he can't hold a candle to you."

"I better scat." He kisses the side of my head. "See you at City Hall."

I shut the door behind him and heave a sigh.

"Your parents are so cute, renewing their vows, and all." Rosie walks out of the kitchen with a glass of her favorite herbal iced tea. Her very pregnant belly makes her waddle as she closes the distance and hands a second glass of regular sweet tea to me. "How cool that you get to be part of it."

"For sure." I sip the cool liquid, wishing I felt more enthusiastic. This is a big deal for them and I don't want anything to go wrong. "It's going to be fun."

"I can't wait to see what's inside that time capsule." Fern, her tiny chihuahua, sniffs around our feet. "Is it okay for me to take my lunch at one so I can watch your mom dig it up?"

"We can go together." All three of my cats are in the right display window, constantly shifting to stay in the beams of sun filtering through the current exhibit of my wedding gowns. Moxley, Logan's basset hound, lifts his head from his bed in my office. He's been staying with me since Logan is spending his days out of town. I scratch Arthur by his ear, and return to my desk to check my schedule again. Moxley flops back over and starts snoring. "Our first appointment is at two-thirty. We should return before then."

Tabby, the marmalade cat who happens to be my ancestor and one of the original founders of the town, yawns and jumps down from her perch. She hops onto the desk and sits on the planner, blocking my view. Her golden eyes narrow at me and she meows.

"What?" I attempt to shift her out of the way, but she hisses, rears her tail in the air and paws at today's date.

Rosie chuckles. "She wants to go, too."

"No," I tell my great-grandmother many times removed. A witch, she's also a shapeshifter, and a troublesome one at that. "You don't need to be running around downtown during the celebration."

A flick of her tail, along with something akin to a growl, and she launches off the desk and heads for the kitchen.

"You know where she's going," Rosie teases.

"Out the doggie door." I think about chasing after her, but know it'll do no good. The woman has some serious magick juju. "How long ago was that time capsule buried?"

Rosie scoops up Fern and sways back to her seat. "When they set the foundation of City Hall back in 1757."

Is it possible Tabitha was there when it went into the ground?

My desk phone rings and I shove the thought aside. "What do you wear to a time capsule reveal?" I half-joke.

"If you're pregnant, maternity clothes," she quips.

I pick up the handset. "The Wedding Chapel & Ava's Events —from flowers and food to the happy 'I dos.' How may I help you?"

"Ava!" Jenn Calhoun's familiar voice is shaking. "You'll never guess what happened!"

Jenn is one of my brides who's getting married next month. She also began working part-time for me recently to cover the cost of her dress, and is scheduled to assist with the upcoming Webster family reunion. "Please tell me your water didn't break."

This gets Rosie's attention and her brows shoot up to her hairline. Jenn is farther along than my office manager, and looks like she'll pop any day.

"No, no, not that." She makes a squealing noise. "Jeremy is coming home early! Next week, in fact. He got a promotion and he'll be here for two weeks before they ship him back out for training in Florida."

"That's awesome." I'm already rearranging tasks in my head. "You'll need time off to be with him then."

"Yes, but more importantly, we need to move up the wedding!" She squeals again.

My stomach bottoms out. I've designed a special edition dress for her, and had planned to marry her and her beau in the backyard next month, but the design isn't finished, and neither are the other preparations. "Um, of course. We'll have to rearrange a few things, and—"

"I can't believe it!" Her excitement practically lights up the phone line. "I'm getting married next week!"

I hate to ask, but have to. "What day exactly did you have in mind?"

"It will have to be Saturday," she says, confirming my worst fear. "Jeremy is calling. I've gotta go!"

She hangs up and I stare at the handset.

"What was all that about?" Rosie asks.

"Jenn's boyfriend is home from the Army," I tell her. "They want to marry Saturday."

Rosie's face falls. "Oh boy. We need to clone you."

I drop the handset into the cradle and sink into my chair. "If you know how to do that, please give me the recipe."

She picks up her phone. "I'll call Gloria to see if she can fast-track the dress. We'll work it out."

That is the least of my worries. Jenn hired me to officiate her wedding as well. Mama and Daddy's isn't until four in the afternoon, so maybe I can get Jenn to hold hers earlier.

"Right," I say to Rosie with more conviction than I feel. "We'll work it out."

❦　2　❦

The day is clear and warm for early May. A gentle breeze lifts the ends of my hair as I walk to my car. Across the way, Logan's Porsche is gone, and I'm disappointed. Just seeing his tousled blond hair and pretty blue eyes would give me a boost right now.

Once I'm in the driver's seat, I text to let him know I miss him. I punctuate it with red lips. He sends a heart in return and claims he'll be home at seven.

I'm not a cook, but we're tired of pizza and sandwiches. We've eaten at the Beehive Diner so much recently, Queenie, the owner and Mama's best friend, has offered us stock in the place. My mother, no matter what else she had going, always insisted we eat dinner together, and while it often was nothing more than mac-n-cheese or hamburgers, she did her best to feed me home-cooked meals. I've recently teased a few of her best recipes from her and have begun making them. Tonight, I plan to whip up some chicken and dumplings with a side of biscuits.

As I wait for Rosie to close and carry Fern to the car in her large tote, I roll down the window to let in fresh air.

What will I say at the ceremony? Since my parents were separated for many years due to a stupid family curse, I missed out on a lot of memories with both of them present. I may be grown, but I'm thrilled they're together once again, and I want Saturday's event to go perfectly.

It takes a minute for Rosie to get settled, wrangle the seatbelt, and situate Fern on her lap. Her belly nearly pushes the tiny dog off, but Fern is getting used to it and manages to maneuver into an agreeable position.

"Perfect day for this, isn't it?" Rosie comments, as I drive around the cul-de-sac. Birds sing in the woods beyond and we curve back past Logan's. "Did Miss Dixie order this weather?"

The Wedding Chapel now sports my new sign with *Ava's Events* hanging on the wrought iron fence. I admire it as Tabby sits on the front porch between the two gargoyles with cat faces at the tops of the railings. Her tail twitches and I smile at her and wave as we pass. "I'm sure she did. She wouldn't allow anything to ruin this occasion. She's been planning it for months."

The Victorian era street lamps and historic buildings that line the road are reminders of an earlier century. I turn south to head to Main Street, various trees and bushes flowering white and pink, adding to the place-out-of-time feeling.

It's one of Thornhollow's calling cards, inviting folks to return to a simpler time. "What do you think they'll find in the time capsule?" I muse.

"No idea. Could be anything." She has her phone and does a search. "The colonies in 1757 sound a lot like now—wealthy people had luxuries, the poor had very little. But hey, the first chocolate factory opened a year prior, so there's that."

"Priorities, right?"

We share a laugh. "This says men wore breeches, stockings, linen shirts, and waistcoats. Tri-cornered hats were popular. Women had corsets made of whale bone"—she makes a face—"and hooped petticoats under their dresses, but, huh, interesting. They didn't wear panties!"

Thinking of Tabitha without underpants is an image I could

do without, especially since I've already seen her buck-naked on more than one occasion. She is anything but modest when she shifts into her human form. "That's screwy, isn't it?."

"I'd feel weird without underwear," she states.

"Can you imagine how unpleasant that clothing would be?"

"Thank goodness fashion has changed since then." She pets Fern and fidgets in her seat. Getting comfortable isn't easy for her anymore, no matter what position she's in. "Do you think there will be anything specific from your grandparents?"

Samuel Thornton and Tabitha Holloway led an exciting life, and not because of what they did or didn't wear. According to the town's history, they were exiled from Colonial Williamsburg for their non-puritan beliefs, and the fact Samuel, a constable, left his family for her.

The truth is significantly different. His first wife, Redemption, was a part of the Salem witches. Her family left there during the trials, even though they'd blended in so well with the Puritans no one realized they were the ones performing magick. Redemption's family were masters at the Craft, and were able to conceal their real nature and turn all eyes on innocent people.

Eventually, my grandfather uncovered this truth and left her. He did his utmost to get their kids away from her, and that's when she turned the town against him.

Tabitha helped Sam escape before the citizens could hang him. Redemption cursed him and his future offspring, while putting protective charms on their children, so he and Tabby could never get them away from her.

All of it was an unheard of thing in that time. Sam and Tabby simply combined their last names to give birth to a new place, and while those who settled here later insisted Samuel and Tabitha were married, there are no records regarding it.

Personally, I don't care. My ancestors had their own family and created a supportive community, free to everyone no matter their religious beliefs or walk of life. I'm proud of that. "I sure hope so. Wouldn't it be fun to discover Samuel's favorite mug or a piece of Tabby's jewelry?"

"You could wear it when you marry Logan!"

I feel my excitement rising to match hers. "That would mean a lot to me. I want to incorporate one of Aunt Willa's scarves into the dress, too."

"It's going to be so cool," she says, squeezing my arm as I pull into the parking lot on the side of the courthouse. News crews are lining the street and Mama is already on the steps, adjusting the podium's microphone and waving at someone in the crowd.

After parking, I assist Rosie out and we walk toward the hub of the event. She tucks Fern into her tote again and the dog disappears.

Logan's mother sees me and nods. "Hello, Ava." Helen looks me over from head to toe, and as usual, I have the sense I fall short of her expectations. "I wasn't sure you were going to make it."

"Lovely day, isn't it?" I echo Rosie's earlier comment and ignore my future mother-in-law's fault finding. I've learned it's part of her nature, and I can't blame her for wanting the best for her son. He's an amazing guy, and while I am lacking in many areas, I love him as much as she does.

Besides, Mama raised me to be polite at all costs, and I know Helen's miffed about my parents holding their party at the Nottingham Hotel instead of her winery. "This is quite the turnout."

Several brand new shovels gleam where they are lined up along the City Hall's historic steps. Red bows on the handles blow in the breeze, and multiple members of the Council and Chamber hover nearby, posing for pictures and offering sound bites to the reporters from the Thornhollow *Tribune*, as well as radio and TV stations.

When Baylor spots me, she rushes over. "Ava, are you prepared for your portion of the unveiling?"

Not really. I'd be happy to turn it over to her. "What do need me to do?"

Her curly brown hair blows around her face, getting in her eyes. She tries to corral it and laughs when a lock flies across her lips. "Support your mother, of course, and"—she delves into her blazer pocket and hands a folded paper to me—"remind folks about the city wide sidewalk sales and specials. Also the special display at the library."

I open the note to find a list of shops and their Founder's Day deals. "I have to speak?"

"You'll do fine," Rosie tells me with a wink.

Helen sniffs. "You're a leader in this community, Avalon, and one of the descendants of Samuel and Tabitha. Straighten that spine and make us proud."

She marches away and Rosie gives me a "whoa" look. She spots a friend who waves at her. "Good luck. Knock 'em dead."

Off she goes to talk to her friend. Baylor smiles knowingly at Helen's back. "Well, guess we know who *wasn't* invited to speak today."

We share a chuckle. "No, she's right. I can handle this,"—I wave the list—"and I do need to *step up and be counted*, as Mama always says." I've grown to love my hometown more than I ever thought I could and I want our community to be a strong one. "Thank you for making my job as president so much easier, Bay. I appreciate you."

She blushes, but can't hide her happy smile. "I devoted the whole front section of the library to your ancestors," she informs me with a hint of pride in her voice. "All the books and maps from that time period, and the local history editions, too. I wanted the copy of Tabitha's journal you gave the Historical Society, but Louise wouldn't loan it to me. Buster says she's a dried up old raisin, just like her artifacts."

Louise Dillion took over after my former neighbor Preston Uphill killed Aunt Willa and attempted to do the same to me. She's a much better person than he ever was, but a stickler for the items she believes should be showcased at her organization for the town to enjoy. Baylor wants them displayed at the library during certain times of the year to make them more accessible to all, and the two would be incredible collaborators if they could work together. Unfortunately, Louise doesn't play well with others, and Baylor's brother, Buster, is quite protective of her feelings. "As soon as I have time to make another copy, I'll get it to you."

"That would be great! I was hoping we might discover something for the library in the time capsule, but even if there is a book or journal, Louise will claim it for the Society."

"I'll talk to Mama," I assure her, seeing Daddy's head over her shoulder as he ambles toward us. "We'll make sure you get a copy of anything you want."

Her smile is filled with relief and she tugs a wayward strand of hair from her eyes again. "More people visit the library than they ever do the Society, and that's how it should be. We have to bring history to the people, not force them to search for it in some musty old mansion."

The library is probably as old as the Historical Society, but I know what she means. She's updated and renovated the place during the past five years whenever there were funds, while the Society's gothic revival hasn't been touched except for the rare maintenance on it.

"Oh, look!" She points toward the parking lot. A tall, thin man with a handlebar mustache unfolds himself from the front of a sedan. "That must be Amos Butterfield!"

I shade my eyes and watch as one of the council members greets him and leads him to the City Hall steps.

Daddy joins us, kissing my cheek. "Hello, Baylor. How are you today?"

She squeezes my arm. "Quite well, thanks to your daughter. You raised her right, Mr. Fantome."

He grins. "I surely tried, but the real reason she turned out so good is due to that woman up there."

He points to Mama who's watching us—*him*. Her face lights up when he waves at her.

"You two are like a couple of high school sweethearts again," I say with mock disgust.

Daddy laughs. "It's good to be home."

Baylor excuses herself. "I have to talk to Mr. Butterfield. He's doing a signing for us of his latest book on Thursday evening. I hope you'll both come."

"Of course," I tell her, making a mental note to add it to my calendar.

Mama motions for me to join her. "The queen beckons," I tell Daddy.

He pats my back. "Catch up with you later."

I join Buster, our city administrator, and Louise behind the podium. "The Society's collection will grow today," Louise comments, rubbing her hands together. She's wearing a vintage black dress that reminds me of a Victorian funeral and a matching hat with lace. "There's going to be something amazing in that time capsule, I can feel it in my bones."

Someone has placed a large sign over the limestone in the lawn a few feet from where it's buried, making sure everyone knows it's location. The oldest tree in Thornhollow, a giant beech, has protected the sight for the past three hundred years. I keep my comment neutral. "It's definitely exciting."

Amongst the onlookers, I spot Helen, Queenie, her son Brax, and his partner Rhys. Queenie waves, Brax whistles, and Rhys gives me a thumbs-up. I know most in the crowd, too, seeing at least one representative from all the families who consider themselves movers and shakers.

"I thought you would change into something more..."— Mama speaks between smiling teeth and guides me into the lineup—"professional."

I keep my voice low. "I'm wearing a dress, Mama. A nice one, in fact. What exactly were you expecting?"

She touches my hair, running her fingers through the tips and fluffing the ends. "Perhaps not gray. It isn't your color, dear." She squeezes in between me and Buster. "Now, smile."

At her signal, the editor from the paper, a tall, lean man named Walter Lee steps forward, camera in hand. He often covers all the *Tribune*'s positions, including reporter. "Everyone, on three. One...two...three."

We smile in unison and Mama insists he take several more shots to be sure at least one is perfect. Mr. Lee doesn't seem to mind, even when she insists he show her the photos and let her pick which she wants to be included in the writeup. "Yes, Miss Dixie," he says in his slow, Southern voice. "Whatever you think is best."

How many times have I said *that* in my life?

Mama introduces Mr. Butterfield to me. He's cool, reserved, but his eyes take in everything. He has one of his mystery novels in hand. "Quaint little town," he says to us with a Texas drawl.

He's the state historian? "You aren't from Georgia, are you?" I ask.

Mama cuts in, giving me a hard frown, and then proceeds to go on and on about how wonderful it is here. Mr. Lee positions us on two rocking chairs on the side of the deep veranda, and the author makes sure his book is in the shot. Mama hovers and then Mr. Lee offers to do another photoshoot later at the Society with Louise, Buster, and Mama next to the items we uncover today.

"That would be lovely," Mama gushes.

Butterfield looks mildly disinterested. "If someone will provide me with directions, I'll be there."

Once that's finished, Reverend Stout joins us and Mama gathers us in a semi-circle. She outlines the itinerary to be sure we're all on the same page. "The minister will say a prayer, I will then welcome the audience and introduce those of us on stage. I'll use a ceremonial shovel to break the soil, then Buster and two city workers will remove the stone and begin digging in earnest."

The City Hall bell peels off the one o'clock hour and Mama takes the podium, shushing the crowd. Reverend Stout steps forward and leads everyone in prayer, giving thanks to the founders and those who came after, and ending with a blessing on all of us.

Mama recites the town's true history, learned from the diary I found in Aunt Willa's attic at Halloween. I'm glad the old stories have been put aside and the truth has been made public. "We believe this capsule was originally intended to be opened a century after its burial, but the paperwork was lost and no one knew it was even here until fifty years ago. The Historical Society found a record mentioning it, but at that time, our city leaders weren't that enamored with the idea. I've been curious about it from the moment I became mayor, and I hope you're all as curious as I am to see and touch a true piece of our town's history!"

Cheers and whistles fill the air. Some clap.

Louise gets in her five minutes about the Historical Society's role in the preservation of the contents, making sure to emphasis her own importance as head of the organization. Then it's my turn to push support for the local small businesses.

As the last of the clapping dies away once I'm done, Mama and Buster walk down the steps and she picks up a shovel. "Here's to Thornhollow, past, present, and future!"

The crowd goes crazy and Mama sends the blade into the ground.

3

Mama stomps her heeled shoe on the metal and sends the blade deeper. The stone over the capsule wiggles slightly. She scoops up a shovelful of soil next to it, and I blink, wondering if it was my imagination or if perhaps she bumped it.

She piles the dirt to the side, beaming, and I clap along with the others, then watch as the city crew closes in to help Buster move the heavy rock marker.

Folks cluster, chatting and speculating about what might be revealed. Reverend Stout stands next to me. "How are you today, Ava?"

"Busy as ever," I tell him. "Keeps me out of trouble."

He chuckles, looking a bit haggard in the spring sunshine. I wonder if the ghost that's been haunting him is keeping him and his wife up at night again. "Idle hands and all that, right?"

"That's what Aunt Willa always preached." In February, he helped me lay a soul to rest at the Nottingham Hotel, but picked up a spectral hitchhiker who has been playing havoc with his wife's organ, as well as the one at the church. No good deed goes unpunished. "Have you had any late night concerts recently?"

The good pastor doesn't believe much in ghostly visitors, so I've had a devil of a time convincing him I need access to the spirit in order to get the man to cross over. Stout believes he can pray the ghost into heaven, I guess, but Mama says he's just stubborn and fears my mediumship gift. I don't blame him; I don't always feel that comfortable with it either.

"I heard your parents are renewing their vows," he deflects.

Gossip travels in our small town faster than the speed of light. "I only learned about it this morning, but yes, they think their thirtieth is the perfect time to do so."

The stone finally gives up its seal with the ground revealing raw orange dirt under it. The men move it to the side of the building, the weight of it seemingly heavier than expected. It takes three of them to lug it out of the way.

"What time will the ceremony be held?"

I hear a tightness in his voice and a trickle of dread sets up in my stomach. "The party is set to begin at four, so I imagine we'll give everyone time to get settled before we do the vows, probably around four-thirty."

More dirt and clay form a pile near the base of the tree, as the digging takes place in earnest. "I understand you'll be performing the service."

Yep, he's definitely unhappy and restraining himself from saying he's hurt and/or offended Mama didn't ask him to do the honors. How do I smooth this one over?

The spring leaves on the ancient tree rustle in the wind, and I trace a scar on the trunk with my eyes. From some dark recess of my memory, I recall that it was struck by lightning a hundred or so years ago, splitting it in two. The town believed it was lost and made arrangements to cut the remaining piece down, but when the removal crew came, they found a new tree growing up from the center. "My parents thought it would be a nice touch to have me handle it, and Daddy and I want to keep the mayor happy," I offer lightly with a wink.

He crosses his arms, cradling his well-worn Bible in the crook of one. "I've been meaning to speak with you about your role as an officiant. I know it's part of your wedding package service, but you aren't a true minister, Ava."

And there's the crux of the matter. "I'm licensed to perform marriages in the state and registered with the county and city. I'm not counseling folks on their spiritual practice or the after-life—that's your area, Reverend. I'm simply making sure they're legally united under Georgia law."

My voice rises and Mama shoots me a disapproving look. There's never a good time to go head to head with a minister, but right now might be the worst.

A shovel hits something harder than the packed earth and a dull clang rings out. "Got something here, ma'am," Slim Cady calls, tossing down his shovel and wiping at the item in the hole.

I use the interruption to move away from the minister and peer down. The crowd's rowdiness hushes and all eyes turn to Slim.

Mama steps forward, eyeing the opening. From my spot peeking over the railing, I see what appears to be dirty concrete.

"We've hit pay dirt, folks!" She announces. "The time capsule is inside a secure box, according to our records, and I believe we just found it!"

The crowd calls "hurray" and applauds. Slim and Buster use their hands to claw at the dirt near the edge of the concrete container. It's bigger than I expected.

Reverend Stout is suddenly by my side again. "I'd appreciate you having respect for the fact I spent years in the seminary, and have been a minister for more time than you've been on this earth."

Louise flies down the steps and squints over Buster's shoulder. I keep my gaze on the proceedings, my mind trying to come up with the right words. This is so unlike him, and while I certainly want us to stay friends, I won't be bullied into dropping my service. "Reverend Stout, you know I have nothing but the highest regard for you and your crucial role in our town, but there are couples who don't want a formal church wedding or have alternate religious beliefs. I respect those, too." I pivot and put a hand on his arm. "In this day and age, many wish to have a family member or best friend unite them, and I find that lovely. I'm no different than one of them—I offer to perform the vows if they want. Again, their spiritual life is not my area of expertise, and I don't offer guidance when it comes to that."

The corner of his eye twitches. He leans close and speaks between clenched teeth. "But you talk to spirits."

I'm slightly taken aback. While he doesn't like the idea I'm a medium, he's never seemed genuinely appalled by it. "I do, and so did Aunt Willa. She was also an officiant. You didn't have issues with her."

Buster, Slim, and the other man tug at the box. The crowd closes in, some attempting to watch over each other's shoulders, jostling for a good view. "Your aunt..." He trails off for a moment and blinks. "You..." Another hesitation and a blink. His face pales, looking almost ashen, and his pupils dilate.

"Reverend?" I grip his arm, "Are you okay?"

As if my touch burns, he jerks away and staggers backward. "Abomination!" he cries, the word echoing across the lawn and the gathered spectators.

Guess where everyone's attention goes now? Yep, straight to me. He stumbles down the stairs, past Louise, who draws back as if he's contagious, and scans the crowd with wild eyes.

Mama tilts her head in confusion. "What's wrong?" she asks him before her gaze turns to me. "What happened?"

I lift my hands in an *I don't know* gesture, and Stout ambles through those gathered like a drunken man, crashing into people and nearly toppling over Sissy Walters' stroller. Her baby starts to cry and Daddy steps from his place on the lawn and takes the man's elbow. "Let's find you a seat." He calls over his shoulder, "Can someone get the vicar some water, please?"

Detective Landon Jones, in his tan police uniform, strides forward to help, but our minister shakes Daddy off, shifting on unsteady feet to point at me. "She's an abomination!"

A loud gasp goes up from quite a few and I feel Mama's incredulous glare land on me. Reverend Stout takes off at a clumsy run and I shrug at the accusatory looks that shoot my way. *I can't wait for that to be on the news tonight.*

I notice Helen cringing behind a hand. Mama sighs loud enough for me to hear, then the mayor in her kicks back in as the men give a final grunt and the container breaks free of the dirt that's been holding it for three hundred years. One corner is crumbling, but it appears to be roughly three by three feet, and at least a foot deep. "Here it is," she says, clapping.

The cheers that go up this time are fewer and less robust, but the attendees nearest to the hole once more jockey for a better view. Daddy says something to Jones, who nods, then he motions to me that he's going to follow Stout. I nod to him as well.

Louise leaves the steps and shoves her hands in white archival gloves. "Don't touch anything inside once you pry it open," she explains to the men. "The contents must be protected from finger oils, and any photographs, documents, or artworks handled with extreme care."

Mama points. "Let's move it to the veranda. Louise can hold up the items, I'll announce what they are, and Ava can document them."

Happy to fade into the background again, but worried about the minister, I accept the tablet Candace shoves at me. "When did you get here?"

She's in a filly pink skirt with a white jacket and I wonder how that's more professional than my sleek gray dress. Her red hair is piled on top of her head and she smiles patiently, as though I'm a child. "I've been here all along, Ava." She points to the device. "Record each item in the spreadsheet and be sure to hit save after you enter them."

With my peripheral vision, I notice Butterfield ogling her from head to toe.

"Maybe you should do it," I say.

"You heard the mayor, she wants you to." With that she

wheels around and disappears through the front doors. Butter-field looks around and slips in after her.

"Okay," I mutter.

Mr. Lee moves quickly, snapping photos of the mostly intact box. Buster accepts a hand trowel from Slim to pry at the lid. Another chunk of concrete breaks free from the damaged corner and Louise nearly has a stroke. "Careful!"

"Sorry," Buster says. His face is flushed, but he's grinning. "I'm just excited."

Snap, snap, goes Lee's camera. Mama, always ready for a publicity shot, slides closer and pats his shoulder. "We all are."

Buster eases the metal edge into the muddy gap, sweating with the effort of cracking through it. A slender piece of clay breaks and the lid lifts an inch on one side.

The breeze rustles the leaves, and I find I'm holding my breath, along with everyone else. It isn't every day you get to see an event like this. Something deep inside me recognizes this is more than just a marketing promo for our town on Founder's Day. This is my heritage. My ancestors formed this town and, even though one still hangs out with me in cat form, I'm directly tied to what's inside. I feel it in my blood, my bones.

As Buster and Slim exchange positions, Buster now has an easier time of breaking the seal. After he goes all the way around, the lid is ready to be removed.

The three men grasp their respective sides, and Mama moves to handle the fourth. She counts to three and they heave in unison.

"They really shouldn't do this."

Persephone's voice makes me jump. I glare at her, but realize I have to act as if she's not here since there are at least fifty people watching this and some are already keeping an eye on me after the Stout incident. "What are you doing here?" I mutter from the corner of my mouth.

My guardian angel is in a robin's egg blue jumpsuit. Her hair is in two long braids with ribbons woven in. No one can see her but me. "You're going to need my help."

They set the heavy lid aside and rush back to where Louise is already peering at the contents. The men carry the container onto the porch, Louise belting out instructions. They place it on a table next to the podium to display the contents.

Louise hands Mama a set of white gloves like hers. "It appears there's a pewter lining," she announces, and fiddles with it a moment before lifting an interior lid. I hear *oohs* and *ahhs* from all four as they survey the contents, but what I'm staring at isn't anything I expected to see.

Rising from the box is a gauzy gray substance I'm all too familiar with. "Oh no," I mutter.

"Exactly," Persephone replies.

The spirit seems to stretch, his essence growing bigger as he fills out. He's wearing clothes like Rosie described on the way here—stockings, breeches, a waistcoat. He's clean-shaven except for a slim mustache and sideburns, and his long hair is pulled back in a bun at the base of his neck. His dark eyes land on me as he floats above the table.

"Who is he?" I ask.

Persephone makes an exaggerated rolling motion with her hand as she extends it in his direction. "Ava, meet your tenth—or is it eleventh? Hmm. Anyway, meet your grandfather. That is Samuel Thornton."

＄ 4 ＄

Louise's eyes grow large. "There's a note!"

Mama removes it and smiles as she holds it up for the crowd to see. She steps to the podium, unrolling the parchment. "The words of our forebears! Listen up, everyone."

You could hear a leaf drop as those gathered fall silent.

"Why, this is quite unsettling," Samuel says. No one hears him but me and Persephone, but his voice sounds nasally and his vowels are drawn out. He scans the people, a deep furrow in his brow. "I do believe I have been asleep for a very long time."

"To the descendants and immigrants of our fair town," Mama reads, "we offer this contribution to the history and observance of our lives, the original founders and citizens of Thornhollow. Upon the opening of these recorded items a hundred years from this day in history, we offer this simple message: a map of our community, that you may see the beginnings of the dream."

She glances at Louise and the woman carefully picks through the contents and her eyes light up as she locates the item. "Here it is." She holds up another aged parchment and unfolds it for all to see. It tries to curl in on itself, and I doubt it's big enough for anyone to get a good look at the sketch of the town at that time, but it will be on display soon for those who care to gander at it.

"Fascinating." She gently lays it on the table. "This is just... such an amazing day!"

Mama nods, grinning, and continues. "A telescope, that you may always look to far shores."

Again, Louise dives inside and retrieves the piece. It's black with gold rings on the ends, and she struggles to get it to extend. When it does, she peers through it and laughingly says, "I spy!"

The men and women laugh with her before she sets it on the table. Samuel hovers in midair, the expression on his face perplexed.

"Ava?" Mama has turned away from the microphone and is staring at me with a frown on her face. "Are you getting these down?"

"I, uh..."

Samuel glances at me and sees me watching him. His gaze takes in my dress, my heels. "You are most unusual."

Persephone chuckles. "You ain't kidding, there, pops."

Gee, thanks. I nod at Mama. "Got 'em right here," I lie, pointing to the tablet.

Sam seems curious about it, about everything. He studies the deep porch ceiling, painted a haint blue to keep spirits away. Lot of good that did. His eyes roam to the giant tree, the sign. "My gracious. What has happened here?"

Mama smooths her frown and smiles before returning to the mic. "A compass, that you shall be able to find your way home, should you ever stray."

Louise repeats pinpointing the object and showing it off. The compass is bigger than a pocket watch and set in bronze. "The detail is exquisite," she tells us.

"Seeds," Mama continues. "While these will be long past their prime, may they remind you to plant your dreams in fertile soil and may your harvest always be prosperous."

Folks clap and whistle. Louise is frowning at the box. Absent-mindedly, she displays a drawstring bag, but her focus isn't on it.

Mama rolls on. "And finally, a bottle of whiskey." This draws hoots and cat-calls. "May you always have a good drink ready for a friend, and find sustenance should you be the friend in need."

Sam's mustache quivers in a crooked grin.

Gingerly, Louise withdraws the bottle and sunlight shimmers through the amber liquid when she holds it up. Her attention, however, is still on what's inside the time capsule.

"Can we sample that?" A man at the front of the gathering cranes his neck to eye the liquor.

Mama waves him off. "Finally, the below signatures of those who have contributed to this collection. We offer an invisible, but earnest blessing, on the town and its inhabitants on this day, 1 May, in the year of our Lord 1757. May you all live long and prosper."

Members of the crowd give the Vulcan salute. She recites the names, oblivious to Louise flicking concerned glances between her and the box.

Samuel's name, as well as Tabitha's, are included. I'm so busy watching him as he inspects the porch, looks in the windows of the building, and once again eyes me, I ignore the crawling sensation running down my spine.

A cat's meow draws my attention and I whip my head around to see Tabby emerging from behind the tree. "Super," I mumble. As usual, she's done what she wants and showed up anyway.

She pads over to the hole, her paws sinking in the freshly-turned dirt. Her marmalade head tips and her neck cranes to see inside.

Samuel floats off the porch, paying no attention to her or any of us. He stares off into the distance and passes right through Detective Jones and several others on the sidewalk. Jones visibly shivers and his dark skin pales.

"Wait!" I call to Sam and everyone looks at me, including Mama.

Over her shoulder, she once more gives me a silent, but chastising glare. "Ava, what is it?"

"Don't worry," Persephone tells me. "He won't go far."

I'm ready to run after him. "How can you be sure?"

Mama screws up her face, then seems to have a sudden revelation. "No, no, no. Not here," she grinds through gritted teeth. She hates it when I see dead people.

Tabby hops into the hole and another meow echoes up out of it. Persephone watches her. "He's bound to this land. He's not going anywhere."

"Um, mayor?" Louise asks tentatively.

"Yes, Louise?" Mama swings toward her. "What is it?"

"I don't know if this is supposed to be in here, but..." She points and Mama leans over cautiously, as if a dead animal might be inside.

"Oh dear," I hear her say. Her head jerks up and she scans the crowd. I know she's searching for Daddy.

Tabby digs furiously, and I rush to glance over the railing. Under her paws, I see something old and stained emerging.

"What is it?" A woman in the crowd calls. "What's in the box?"

Several folks walk to the steps. Buster waves them back. "Now, now, you'll all get to see the items on display later at the Society's open house."

Mama motions for Detective Jones to join us on the porch. He shuffles up the steps. "What's wrong, mayor?"

She points to the box's interior.

"Well, I'll be," I hear him utter. "What do we have here?"

Tabby glances up, sees me watching her. Her tiny paws fly through more dirt and clay and then she steps back. Her golden eyes beseech me to look.

Mama hands Detective Jones one of her gloves and he dons it. He reaches into the container and lifts out the final item.

A knife with a wooden handle and a six-inch blade appears. It's wrapped in a dark stained cloth. "This isn't on the list, I take it?" Jones asks Mama.

She shakes her head, lips pressed into a line.

"Wow," the man who wanted the alcohol says. "Is that dried blood?"

Murmurs race through the group. From his pocket, the detective pulls out an evidence bag, sliding the knife inside.

At the same time, I glance back to see what Tabby has uncovered. My stomach clenches and I feel slightly woozy. "Detective Jones?"

"Yes?"

When I motion to him, he closes the bag and moves to my side. I point and he peers at Tabby and the hole.

"Huh. This is turning out to be quite a day," he intones.

Others now follow the direction of our gazes. Down below, a skull and bones lay half revealed in the dirt.

$\maltese$ 5 $\maltese$

They're old, even I can tell that. The person they belong to has been dead a long time, and I have a sneaking suspicion I know whose they are.

Detective Jones, eager to be the official expert, insists the time capsule, its contents, and the entire front of City Hall, including the dig site, be cordoned off and treated as a crime scene "until further notice." He chases Tabby away and she hisses at him.

Louise argues that she needs photographs of the items, and while Jones, Mama, Buster, and some of the townsfolk wait for crime scene technicians from the county to arrive, the detective allows Mr. Lee to shoot pictures as long as no one touches the artifacts.

I've moved to stand under the tree, a few feet from the yellow tape now cordoning off the lawn and front steps. Mama is busy handling the news outlets and the endless questions everyone throws at her.

I see Rosie ambling over, her focus on me. I speak as well as I can without moving my lips to my guardian angel. "How is it my grandfather is buried there?"

Persephone sits on a low tree branch, swinging her legs.

"This is more fun than that true crime channel. He definitely lived a fascinating life."

Rosie's nearly to me and I lower my voice to a whisper. "Would it kill you to give me a direct answer? Does this have anything to do with Redemption's curse?"

"What else?" she retorts.

"I can't believe it." Rosie sidles up to me, cheeks flushed. She crosses her arms over her belly and Fern peeks out from her tote. The tiny dog quivers with excitement, or maybe she has to pee. Hard to tell. "A bloody knife inside the capsule? A skeleton under it? I feel like I'm in an Agatha Christie novel."

More like Alfred Hitchcock. "It's certainly interesting, but it might not be anything scandalous." At least, I hope it isn't. "Those bones are probably from some ancient burial and have nothing to do with the time capsule. You know how the land shifts and burps things up."

She turns skeptical eyes on me. "You're hiding something."

I glance around, hoping to see Samuel. Instead, Queenie, Brax, and Rhys head our way. "A ghost came out of the container," I tell her. She's never uncomfortable with my mediumship. "Don't say anything, though, okay? I'm not sure why or what's going on. This day has already gone to the dogs, and I don't want to upset Mama any further."

While Rosie isn't freaked about my ability, and even encourages it, this is a lot to take in. "Are you kidding me?" Her elevated voice draws attention. "That is so cool! What did he—was it a man or a woman?—look like?"

I motion with my hand for her to keep it down. "Shh. Let's not—"

"What did who look like?" Queenie closes the distance to join us, Brax and Rhys on her heels.

"Nobody." I force a smile. "What a day, huh?"

Brax, towering over all of us, rubs his chin. "This is the most excitement Thornhollow has seen in...well, ever, probably."

Rhys is bobbing up and down on the balls of his feet. "That

stuff they left us is pretty amazing, and the note was inspiring. The bloody knife, though? That kinda took the spotlight away from everything else."

"We don't know that's what is on the cloth," I state emphatically.

Queenie glances back. "True, but you've got to admit, it sure appears to be blood."

I'm still holding the tablet, and I search the lingering spectators for Candace. She's half-hidden in the shadows on the side of the building where Mama is still attempting to put a positive spin on all this. "If nothing else, the town will be on every news station tonight." I try for a positive spin too. "I bet we'll see a spike in tourism the rest of the week."

"There's no such thing as bad publicity," Rhys says sarcastically. His blond hair blows in the breeze.

"I need to return this to Candace." I see Tabby darting behind the building and wonder what she's up to. "I'll meet you at the car, Rosie."

The others close rank to keep taking guesses at who the skeleton might be, and I skirt the taped off area to make my way to the horde gathered around Mama. Her cheeks have high color, and I see the strain near her eyes, but the confident smile never leaves her lips.

"I assure you the police will get to the bottom of this," she states, pointing a finger in the air. "As soon as I receive a report with their findings, you'll be the first ones to know."

As she fields another question, I make eye contact with Candace. I quickly finish adding the last couple of pieces as I walk in her direction, but I doubt it's a big deal at the moment. Working my way past the media, I manage to slip in next to her.

"Here's your inventory list," I say in a quiet voice. It certainly wasn't as long as everyone anticipated, but as Rhys mentioned, the included items are fascinating artifacts, and the note from the founders is very motivational. "Tell Mama I'll talk to her later."

She accepts the tablet and holds it up in front of her lips to hide them from anyone watching. "You saw something, didn't you?"

I feign innocence. "Sorry?"

"Don't play dumb." Her eyes dart around. "Everyone knows you see ghosts. You saw one at the grave, didn't you?"

"I saw my cat digging in the hole." I refuse to admit to anything else at this point. I don't need her confronting Mama about it, or spreading gossip. "Speaking of, I need to round her up and get home. Have a good day."

I march away, running into Daddy returning from chasing Reverend Stout. "Hey, what happened?" he asks, surveying the place.

I pull him aside and bring him up to speed. "Unfortunately, from the conversations I've overheard, people have jumped to the conclusion the knife is a murder weapon and was used on the person who's bones are in the ground."

"Wow." He appears as excited as Rosie, the former lawman in him curious as a cat. "That's so cool. Wonder who it is?"

"You all have a warped idea about what's cool," I tease. "How's the reverend?"

"Upset about something. He wouldn't talk to me, and said he wasn't feeling well and needed to lie down. Shut the door in my face."

"Well, you tried. I know he's troubled that I'm performing your vows. Maybe we should find a way to work him into it?"

Daddy nods. "Good idea. He conducted the original ceremony, and I can see that he might feel hurt we're not asking him to do this one. I'll talk to your mother."

"I need to get back to The Wedding Chapel for appointments. Mama's going to have a rough afternoon. If you two want to drop by for dinner, I'm making chicken and dumplings."

He squeezes my arm and kisses my forehead. "Sounds delicious. I'll call you later."

Leaving him, I realize Butterfield is in his vehicle, watching the proceedings. He keeps raising a handheld recorder to his lips and speaking into it. His gaze tracks me as I walk to my vehicle, but I ignore his stare and search for Tabby.

"Here, kitty, kitty," I call. "If you want a ride home, better get your furry backside in the car."

She doesn't show herself, and Rosie waddles over. "Should we look for her?" she asks.

I scan the area, both for her and Samuel, my insides crawling. "She'll be fine," I say, and I hope it's true. "Let's go."

"We need to look for someone," I tell Rosie as we pile in the car.

She rolls her belly forward and Fern jumps down to make a bed on the floor at her feet. "Tabby? She sure knows how to make an appearance, doesn't she?"

"She's on her own to get back to the house." I pull out of the parking spot and take a gander at the grounds, the building, and the nearby park. "I'm searching for my grandfather."

"I thought both your grandfathers were... Oh." Her gaze races around. "You mean...the ghost that came out of the time capsule?"

Persephone pops into the back seat, startling me. "I can't wait to hear what he's got to say when he sees Tabitha."

I ignore her and respond to Rosie. "Samuel Thornton, in fact."

"No." Her hand slaps my arm as I drive down the street. "Seriously? *The* Samuel Thornton?"

I peer between shops, down alleys, and around corners. A car behind me honks and I wave them to pass, since I need to go slow and see if I catch sight of him. "The one and only."

"He's been trapped in there all this time? How awful. Poor guy. Are those his bones? What do you think happened?"

The car passes, the driver giving me a frown and hard glare. I wave and smile, as if I appreciate them passing, then glance in the rearview at Persephone for confirmation regarding my grandfather. She shrugs.

Narrowing my eyes at her, I reluctantly return to surveying Main Street. She can't interfere with my life, only offer the occasional tip to help me deal with ghosts. Sure would be nice if she could at least confirm or deny facts to help me out.

I'm sweating and it isn't even seventy yet. "I assume so. It appears Redemption's curse on the family may have been more layered than I realized. I don't know what's going on with him, but I intend to find out. He obviously hasn't crossed over."

Rosie makes a sound of awe in her throat. "Ava Fantome, you are the most interesting person I've ever met."

The one time the word 'cool' would be appreciated, I get that instead. That term has so many meanings, it's not necessarily a compliment. "Thanks, I think."

She sits forward—at least as much as she can—and braces her hands on her knees. Fern stares at her with adoration, her big, round eyes watery. "What does he look like?"

Her help is appreciated, even though she can't see spirits. "The same as you read from that website description. Straight out of the 1700s, breeches and all."

"Whoa, that's so—"

I hold up a hand. "Cool, I know.

"He should be anchored to his bones," Persephone says. She appears to be scanning the street for him, too. "He can probably only move in a five-mile or so radius of them."

That was still a lot of territory to cover. "If I were Samuel, where would I go?" I ponder.

The answer hits all of us at the same time. Rosie and I exchange a glance, and Persephone echoes our response. "The old homestead."

No longer taking it slow, I stomp on the accelerator. We fly around the corner and I chew my bottom lip. Fern whimpers and Rosie picks her up. She soothes the tiny thing, who tries to climb inside her blouse.

Samuel couldn't care less about the Victorian home that's now where I live and work. My aunt turned her beautiful house into her office, opening the rooms on either side of the grand door to create a big floor space. Each sports a giant bay window where we display wedding themes and other formal party events to showcase our offerings. But at the rear of the one acre rolling property is a stream, and in the northeast corner is the old homestead. *His* house.

The poor two-story is in disrepair after decades of neglect. Previous Thornton-Holloway generations believed in maintaining it, but over the span of three hundred years, the new, more modern structure was built and the empty residence involved too much upkeep. Family members became overwhelmed or lacked interest in it, and long before Aunt Willa became owner of the property, it had been left to fend for itself.

The last renovation happened approximately a century ago, based on the records Aunt Willa kept. Those updates weren't true to the original farmhouse. Portions of rotting woodwork were replaced and the kitchen and master bath wallpapered. A modern kitchen sink instead of the original copper version, which is still upstairs in the attic, and the plain, shaker-style furniture is stuffed up there, too. When the upholstered Victorian chairs and sofas of the main house went out of fashion, they were relegated as well.

The woods near the place have encroached on it, the stream overflowing its banks most springs and nearly reaching the foundation. Animals have used it for birthing babies, and some are especially fond of the stuffed furniture, creating hidey-holes in the seats.

"I do believe he will be dismayed at the state of his former abode," I say in the best imitation I can of my grandfather's voice.

Rosie shoots me a look and giggles. "What kind of accent is that?"

"A bad one, but as close as I can come to how he sounds."

"He spoke to you?"

I turn, spotting The Wedding Chapel. Two of the parking spots are taken by Evander Quigg's red truck, *Quigg Construction* plastered on the sides and tailgate. "He did, but not to me per se. He commented about being freed from the time capsule."

Rosie ogles me for a moment, then points at Evan's truck. "I suppose this is serendipitous."

I don't know about that, but today appears to be one of unexpected surprises. The entire City Council, Chamber, and Historical Society have made it a point to encourage me to fix up the place. It is a monument to our town, and I hate to see the house falling in on itself.

I finally broke down and had an architect friend of Logan's walk through the place with me a few weeks ago. He recommended where to begin the remodel. If we want it to qualify as a historical establishment, and open it to the public, we have hundreds of tasks to perform to bring it up to code. Because of its relevance, however, there is also plenty of grant money available to cover the associated costs.

One of the only local general contractors who specializes in bringing old buildings back to the former glory happens to be Evander and his son, Bisby. Their schedule is tight, but because another job fell through, he offered to start next week.

"What is he doing here?" I have to park across the street at Logan's since my normal spot is taken.

"Guess he can start early," Rosie says.

Better that than not at all. "I'm sure Sam won't be happy to see his farmhouse in disrepair, but at least I can assure him I'm going to fix it up."

Rosie maneuvers Fern into her bag. "Looks like Jenn's here, too."

The pregnant girl is sitting in a rocking chair on the porch. She waves as we get out. Evan and Bis are leaning on the truck, talking to her across the lawn, and they both straighten when they see me and Rosie.

"I'm sorry, Miss Rosie," Evan drawls, tipping his cap to us. He's a medium-sized man with a wide frame. After years of working inside and out, his skin is toast colored and wrinkled, his hair faded to a dusty brown. His matching mustache is sprinkled with a few gray hairs. "I should've parked down the way there. Forgot y'all wouldn't be here 'cuz of the capsule reveal."

He reaches for her hand and helps her on the sidewalk. Bis, a taller, more slender version of his dad, opens the gate and ushers us through.

"No worries," Rosie says. "I'm a whale, but I can still walk a few steps across the street. However, we are expecting clients this afternoon, so it would be better if you didn't hog our limited parking."

"I'll move the truck," Bis tells her with a nod.

As he returns to the vehicle, keys in hand, Evan and I walk beside Rosie to the front porch. "I wasn't expecting you today".

"We had a few minutes to spare before we're due at the county office. Since we have to make a trip there anyway, I thought I'd take some measurements, check on what we need to start on first, so I can file for the corresponding permits."

Jenn comes to her feet and opens the door. She has a key to the place and I'm unsure why she didn't invite the men inside. She and Rosie do a belly bump as their hello to each other, and she pats my shoulder as I guide Rosie in. "I already organized the papers that were on your desk and ordered the supplies for the Macon reunion next month."

We get inside and Moxley, Arthur, and Lancelot greet us. "Wow, you're a busy beaver."

Jenn is practically beaming with eagerness. "Gloria's on her way. We're going to do a dress fitting in an hour."

"Awesome." Another thing I have to squeeze in. I turn to Evan, ready to get out to the homestead and check for grandpa, but manners come first. "Sweet tea?"

"Nah. We just had lunch." In his overalls and ancient leather boots, cracked from years of wear, he seems quite out of place among the wedding supplies and decorations scattered throughout the first floor. "The structure is in the rear, correct?"

I point to the kitchen. "Through there and out the back door. Go down the hill to the stream, you can't miss it. I'll catch up in a minute."

Moxley follows me to my desk. From the bottom drawer, I withdraw the file with all the paperwork for the remodel, from the architect's reconstruction of the original building to the historical register's rules and regulations. "I'll be back as soon as I can," I say to Rosie and Jenn. "This shouldn't take long."

Bis comes in and I motion for him to join me. Moxley sniffs at his pant legs.

"Don't worry about us." Rosie moves her paperweight aside and hands several orders to Jenn. "Go find your... I mean, help Evan."

I walk Bis through the kitchen, making the offer of a beverage to him as well. He waves me off, producing a sports drink from one of his overall pockets. His phone is in his other hand. "Just heard about what happened downtown. Wild, huh?"

We slip through the mudroom to the porch. Mox tags along. "For sure."

Bis holds open the screen door and I lead the dog and him to the backyard and garden.

"Wow, this is nice," he says, as we pass the fountain and rose bushes. Birds greet us with song and the breeze makes the willow tree down the hill trail its slender branches along the ground.

Moxley sniffs everything, taking a moment to mark a tree. I scan for Sam, see no one of the ethereal variety.

Evan has a notebook and pencil and is staring at the foundation, checking the corners, and making notes. "She's a beauty, but she's pretty far gone."

My heart sinks. This was what I was expecting, but I'd still held out hope this might be an easy process. "Can you fix her?"

"That's what I do," he says calmly, making another note. "It will take some time, but the foundation is square and still mostly intact. That's a start. That corner"—he points to the one nearest the creek bank—"is cracked due to moisture over the years, but as old as this gal is, I'm surprised there isn't more damage."

I hand Bis the file and bend to scratch Mox's ears when he lumbers over. "I've made copies of my aunt's notes on the place, and included what the experts say the house looked like when it was built. There's also a rendering of the interior details by an architect who works on restoration projects from this period. If you need anything else, let me know."

A puff of air lifts my hair from the back of my neck, and chills the sweat around my brow. There's no sign of Sam, Tabby, or any other ghost. I'm slightly relieved and also disappointed. I thought this would be the first place he'd visit.

Bis pages through the folder and Evan sketches a drawing, adding an item to a numbered list in his notebook. "We'll be out of your hair in a few minutes. I'm going inside and check the structural walls and roof."

I rub my tingling neck, wondering what's causing it if not a spirit. "Of course. Watch your step. Lots of wood rot and the stair banister is unsafe."

He gives me a patient smile and pockets the notebook. "We'll be careful."

I sigh as the two enter the house, and wonder where Sam has gone. Surely at some point, he'll visit here, won't he? Trouble is, I can't watch it twenty-four seven.

The willow tickles the ground and I think about Aunt Willa.

She'd be thrilled to see this place restored. Turning on my heel, I head for the house. "Come on, Mox."

The dog doesn't follow, giving a lone bark. Looking over my shoulder, I find him staring at the upstairs window.

I glance up, expecting to see Evan or Bis.

My grandfather stares down at me.

$\mathbb{R}$ 7 $\mathbb{R}$

I wave and he draws back, like someone caught spying. Hustling to the tiny porch, Moxley running to keep up, I enter the homestead.

Evan and Bis look up, surprise on their faces. They're inspecting the brick fireplace that's the center of the downstairs and as tall as I am. "Is something wrong?" Bis asks.

Movement above and to the left catches my eye. I see Sam floating down the stairs, his keen gaze on me. "No, nothing." *Only my great-grandfather's ghost floating around.* The spirit in question flies to the bottom and heads into the hall. "I just, uh... remembered I wanted to check something in the back."

Under their quizzical gazes, I smile and vamoose, shifting aside a wooden stool in my way. The back room must have been my grandparents'—when I arrived in Thornhollow last Halloween after Aunt Willa's untimely death, it was where Tabitha shape-shifted into human form the first time I caught her.

Nothing like seeing your great-grandmother naked as a welcome home.

The room is dark, a towering oak outside shading this part of the house from the afternoon sun. Cobwebs hang across the frame and dust motes dance in a slim shaft of wan light when I brush the webs aside. "Careful where you step, Mox," I tell the dog. "Don't get a splinter or nail in your paws. Logan will never forgive me."

The dog leans his stocky body against my calf, sticking to me like glue. I'm not sure if it's a show of solidarity or he's scared. "Samuel?" I whisper, wishing I had a flashlight. "Are you in here?"

The wooden frame of the old bed is stacked on its side and propped against the far wall. A rocking chair rests unmoving in the corner next to a filigreed table that matches the old Victorian furniture in the living room. A dusty oil lamp sits on its scarred surface, the hurricane top missing.

This room seems ten degrees cooler and goosebumps pebble the skin on my arms. There's a matching fireplace in here, only smaller than the main one. "Samuel? I know this must be unnerving to find yourself here." In sync, Moxley and I step deeper into the rectangular space. "I'm Ava, your granddaughter. I can help you."

"This is most unfortunate."

His voice comes from behind me. I whirl, but see nothing.

Then he's there.

Then he's not.

It's like watching a lightening bug hovering over the lawn on a summer night. Spirits often fade in and out, depending on the amount of energy they can leach off the living. Samuel may have had enough from the crowd to stay visible to me, but now his charge is draining.

He flickers back into view, looks down at his body, then up at me. "Pray tell, what is happening to me?"

"You're a ghost." This seems to be news to him and his expression shifts to bewilderment. I've learned there is no easy way to break this kind of news to those souls who don't already know they're dead. "Your spirit has been inside our time capsule for three hundred years."

"Why, that's not possible. I do not understand."

"Neither do I, but—"

Evan calls to me. "Everything alright back there?"

"Yes, fine," I reply automatically, but Samuel flickers out.

Moxley growls. His warm body continues to press against my lower leg.

"It's okay," I soothe both him and my grandfather. "We'll figure it out and get you to cross over."

"Cross over?" Only his words come through now and his tone is incredulous. "Please speak more clearly, child. I have no understanding of that expression."

Where is Tabby when I need her? Or my guardian angel? "Can you meet me at the house up the hill? I can explain things to you there."

"I need...something."

My eyes go the rocking chair where his voice seems to be coming from. "What?"

His spectral body winks in, his gaze on the floor under the table. It rises to stare at the fireplace. "I can feel it calling to me."

"Look, Tabitha is still around and I can get her to assist us with all of this, but I really need—"

"Hey," Bis says behind me, making me jump. He stands in the doorway, surveying the room. "Are you talking to yourself?"

Sam disappears and I smile, attempting to look abashed. I have no idea if the Quiggs have heard gossip about my ghost-whispering skills or not. I've learned it's a lot to drop on someone, especially those who aren't believers, so I keep it to myself when possible. "You caught me. I was just imagining what it must have been like for my ancestors living here, you know? I feel their presence so strongly. It's like they're still here in some ways."

He nods, then points toward the stairs, seemingly oblivious to my play on the truth. "We're heading up to check the second floor and attic. Do you know if those two levels were added after the original structure?"

"From the notes I've gathered, I think the house grew as the family did, so yes, it's probable."

His hand taps the frame. "Awesome. Thanks."

More dust glides through the air. I hear the squeak and groan of dry wood as they ascend. Waiting until I know they're out of earshot, I take a deep breath and wonder what Sam is looking for. "I'm afraid all your possessions are long gone," I tell him.

The temperature drops another degree. He shimmers into being, a hand on the mantel. "No, it's here. I sense the item's presence. I must have it back."

"Why? What is it?"

His face turns so he can look at me. "Who did you say you were?"

"Your granddaughter. My name is Ava."

"I have no recollection of any such name, nor any granddaughter."

"Because we never met." My breath frosts in the chilly air and I shiver. "Like I mentioned, you've been trapped for three centuries."

"I am a spirit?"

"Yes." I feel relief I'm finally getting through. "You need to cross over to the afterlife."

"You called me Samuel."

My relief leaves as fast as it came. "That's your name, isn't it?"

His gaze returns to the fireplace. His essence fades, wobbles. I'm losing him. "I do not know," he states softly, and then he's gone.

The temperature instantly shoots to normal once more. I hear the floor overhead shifting from the Quiggs moving, and the low murmur of their voices filter down to me.

"Samuel?" I call as loudly as I can without them hearing. "I mean, whoever you are, please come back. I can help you find the thing you need." That's probably not true, but I'm desperate not to lose him.

Nothing. I curse under my breath, swearing I will kill my

guardian angel for misleading me. "Maybe you're still related to me, just a descendant of Samuel's, or a brother, or something."

It's possible his ghost wasn't contained at all, it only appeared that way. If he's the ghost of the bones buried under it, it's possible he got stuck in the ground and was simply released at the same time.

Whoever it is could have died before the capsule was buried there, or even afterward. If the person was, indeed, murdered, what better place to conceal the body? What better place than a time capsule to hide the murder weapon?

I reach out a few more times, but get no response. "Come on, Mox. Let's go. This is getting us nowhere."

Back in the main house, I get a glass of sweet tea and hear the lovely voice of Gloria, my seamstress, coming from the living room. She has a delicate French accent and does amazing things with my designs, turning them from pencil sketches into gowns, as easily as waving a magic wand.

"*Allô, ma chérie*," she says when I enter. She's measuring Jenn's bump and has a few straight pins stashed between her lips.

We have an actual fitting area now, after Logan helped me rearrange the living room and put in a raised platform and floor-to-ceiling mirror at the far end.

I take a long drink, letting the cool beverage wash away some of my worry. "Thank you for coming on such short notice, Gloria."

After removing the pins and slinging the red tape around her neck, she hustles over and hugs me. "Anything for you and your beautiful mama-to-be." She stands back and scrutinizes my face. "You look as though you've seen a ghost. Have you?"

"We were telling her about what happened today at the Founder's event." Rosie types away on her laptop, but her eyes glance around the main room. "Is Samuel here?"

"No, and I'm no longer sure he's my grandfather," I tell them. "He either has amnesia or Persephone lied."

At the mention of her name, the angel pops in. "I don't lie. Ever."

I won't give her the satisfaction of glancing at her. "Anyway, ghosts aside, we have a lot on our plate this afternoon."

I eye Jenn in the swaths of white satin circling her ample bosom and the layers of skirt billowing from her non-existent waistline. Her heart is set on my Ella design, which is a fairytale ballgown. She thought it would minimize her full girth, but it seems to have the opposite effect, and she resembles a hot air balloon, ready to float away.

"You know," I say gently, "instead of trying to camouflage your pregnancy,"—which is impossible—"would you consider a different style? One that will spotlight your fantastic shape?"

Her gaze swings to the giant mirror. "Fantastic shape?" She points at herself. "Have you seen me?"

Gloria catches on to what I'm offering. "Ava has a good point. This is a celebration of you, your love for Jeremy, and the child you've created. You should strut your stuff, as they say, show off the baby, rather than downplay the pregnancy."

Jenn chews on her bottom lip. "You think so?"

I touch Gloria's hand. "What about the Ariel? Can we add a yard to the top of the sample you basted together and drop the waist?"

Gloria's eyes twinkle. "Piece of wedding cake!" She laughs at her own joke. "I have yards and yards of fabric in the car. Give me an hour?"

"Wonderful. The sample is upstairs in the guest bedroom closet. Aunt Willa's sewing machine is there, too, if that helps."

She hustles out to her car. Jenn looks doubtful.

I smile at her reflection. "Try it on for me. You don't have to commit to it, but it will be easier to modify in time for this weekend. If you don't want it, we'll do what needs to be done to this one, okay?"

Relief floods her features. She lifts the voluminous skirt and

I help her step down from the platform. "You're the expert. I'll try it."

Persephone hovers in my peripheral vision but doesn't show in the mirror. As Jenn goes to change out of the Ella, I glare at the angel. "You need to tell me the truth about—"

She's saved from the chewing out when Evan and Bis join us. "We'll get out of your hair now," Evan says when he spots me. "Got the measurements we need and an idea of where to begin. It'll be a week before the permits come through, by all accounts, so you probably won't see us until then."

"Sounds good, thank you," I respond and they head to the exit.

Bis stops there and glances over his shoulder at me once his father is outside and going down the porch steps. "I felt them, too," he says quietly, and then he nods and closes the door behind him.

"What's he talking about?" Rosie asks, curiosity lighting her face.

I'm gaping at where he just stood, a dozen questions running through my mind. Is he sensitive to ghosts? Can he see and hear them like I can? "I'm not sure," I respond, turning away. "But I intend to find out."

8

The backyard is alive with the song of evening insects and the birds settling in for the approaching night. A mockingbird serenades me from the top of the gazebo, as I sip a good merlot that came straight from the Cross vineyards.

Logan is running late, which is normal these days, and the chicken and dumplings are warming on the stove. I'm wearing one of Aunt Willa's aprons, covered in flour from the biscuits I made earlier, and I'm sure there's still some on my face and neck, too.

Evenings out here on the porch bring me comfort, as does the wine. I remember when my aunt used to sit here in the evenings while I attempted to catch fireflies.

I feel close to her, like always, but I'm also watching for Samuel. Or Tabby. Neither has made an appearance so far.

My phone rings and I see it's my father. I know what he's going to tell me before I answer. "Hi, Daddy. Is Mama okay?"

"She's tuckered out, I'm afraid. I made her soup and tried to get her to watch her favorite show, but she's glued to the news stations."

I've seen the news too. "Channel 5 claims they're exhuming the body first thing tomorrow."

I hear the squeak of his chair, and imagine him settling in. "Yep, a forensic anthropology expert is being called in to determine how old the skeleton is, and hopefully, how the guy died. I got a glimpse before Jones chased me off. There's a nice sized crack in the skull. He was probably whacked over the head."

A quick internet search told me that bones can determine the person's age, the time of death, and occasionally the presence of a crime. I'm guessing my guardian angel could tell me the same in far less time.

Persephone is AWOL, along with the others, my 'liar' comment causing this cold shoulder treatment, no doubt. "I'm assuming it happened a long time ago, so I doubt the culprit is still around."

"I do love a good cold case, and Jones is already overworked."

His words sink in. "Are you going to help with the investigation?"

"If they need me, sure. Why not? My next out-of-town gig isn't until the end of this month, and recording my upcoming album won't start until the next. I'm writing a few more songs for it, but my schedule's flexible."

Mama will straight up kill him, I imagine, but by the enthusiasm in his voice, there's no stopping him at this point. "Well, those bones aren't going anywhere, and like I said, if there was foul play, I doubt the killer is still alive. Tell Mama to rest, and don't you get so wrapped up in this you aren't prepared for Saturday. We've got a lot to accomplish between now and then."

"About that." The chair creaks again. "Do you have any dresses your mother might be able to wear?"

I set down the glass a little too hard and it clanks on the side table. "A bridal dress?"

"Yeah, you know, nothing fancy, but one that's tailored and sophisticated like she is."

Moxley, who's been lying on the top step perks his ears. I glance around, but see no sign of ghosts. "You do realize that type of design requires fittings and alterations. It's not something Gloria can whip out in a heartbeat."

Although, she kind of did for Jenn and the mermaid-style gown our bride-to-be agreed on. That one is tacked together at the moment, and Gloria will be working on it night and day to finish the final version before the ceremony. I can't possibly ask her to do a second.

"Something in an ivory would be nice," Daddy says, as if he isn't listening to me. "I suggested wearing her original gown, but she says it won't fit in the waist. You know how sensitive she is about her weight. She's planning on wearing a suit, but I was hoping you might be able to help."

There's nothing I wouldn't do for my parents, but I'm at a loss. If I could sew, I might be able to work with Mama's gown, but I'm the designer. I only sketch them, not build them.

There's one that's simple and elegant and Gloria recently convinced me to do a version in off-white. It's part of my latest Roaring Twenties line, and the straight waist might work.

I take a deep breath, refusing to let him, or Mama, down. Surely, there is something I can figure out, and maybe Gloria can give me a quick tutorial on the sewing machine.

Mama calls this streak stubbornness; Daddy says it's competitiveness. I don't know what it is, nor do I care. "Let me look into it."

Mox's head turns and he cocks it, listening. Daddy chuckles. "Thank you, daughter. You're the best."

A second later, I hear the familiar purr of Logan's Porsche coming down the road. "No promises. Altering takes time and we don't have much of that. There should be plenty of chicken and dumplings left tonight. I'll drop some by tomorrow for you."

"Love you, baby girl."

Moxley pushes to his feet, no small act with his chubby body. Luckily, he has short feet and strong legs. He gives a "ruff" and goes to the pet door, squeezing through it.

I grab my glass, take a look toward the old homestead, and follow him inside. "Love you, too, Daddy. Talk tomorrow."

On my way through the kitchen, I turn up the burner on the pot of food. I greet Logan at the front door and he drops his briefcase before hugging me. Then he takes the glass from my hand, downs the last of it, and pets Moxley. "Sorry, I'm late."

His hair is mussed as though he's been running his hands through it, and his tie is askew. I kiss his cheek, unburden him of the empty goblet, and lead him to the kitchen. "Don't worry about it."

The biscuits are cold, so I pop them in the microwave while he grabs two clean glasses and fills them, emptying the bottle. "This case is going to be the death of me."

"Please don't toss that term around lightly," I tease. "There's been enough unexpected and unwelcome surprises around here today as it is."

"I heard about the excitement." He removes the tie and hangs it on the back of a chair, and slouches in another. "Whatever you have cooking smells absolutely amazing and I'm starving."

Tiny crow's feet at the corners of his eyes show his tiredness. I offer the basket of biscuits and he snags one to munch on while I prepare bowls for us. The chicken and dumplings steam when I set them on the table. "It was quite a day."

He descends on the food, making appreciative noises as he eats. "Tell me all about it," he says.

I smile, watching him enjoy the food. I never had much interest in cooking until I had him to feed. Between Aunt Willa's recipes and Queenie's instructions, I'm getting better and find it comforting after a long day. "The time capsule held a knife with a bloody cloth wrapped around it and a skeleton was discovered under the place where it was buried. We really don't know much more than that, except..."

He glances up, seeing my expression as I toy with a biscuit.

"Uh oh. I know that look." He sits back and sips. "Let me guess, you saw a ghost."

"I believe it's Samuel Thornton, but I can't confirm that. Our conversation was brief, but he seems to have amnesia."

Logan frowns. "Is that a thing?"

"No clue. I haven't had time to dig into it—no pun intended. I thought I'd call Winter tonight, and maybe Sage and Raven. One may know if ghosts can get it. My dad had a look at the skull and mentioned it had an unusual crack. Could be from the ravages of time, but it could suggest he was hit with something."

"Sam Thornton is buried in the cemetery, isn't he? His gravestone marker is there. I remember seeing it on our class trip in fifth grade when we did the local history unit with Mrs. Whittler."

I scoop up a bite and eat. "According to all accounts, yes. Another thing I have to check into. Just because there's a headstone doesn't mean he's under it."

"True. Was it weird? Seeing him?"

I swallow and swirl my spoon in the liquid. The dumplings aren't as good as Mama or Queenie's versions, but still tasty. "Sort of, but since I never knew him in life, I'm more curious about him than anything. He was at the homestead and said there was something there he needed. An item, although he couldn't tell me what it is."

I go on to share Persephone's info, claiming he is my great-grandfather and his being trapped in the box is part of Redemption's curse.

Logan takes a second biscuit and breaks it apart. "Curiouser and curiouser. So he could have been stabbed, bludgeoned, or have no connection to the bones at all. He may be your relative who was cursed by his first wife, a Salem witch, or someone else entirely."

"Correct on all accounts, counselor."

"Sounds like a fun mystery."

That makes me think of Sherlock, the ghost who attached

himself to me at the magickal library next to Sage and Raven's Chicks With Gifts Emporium not far from here. He's been helpful with a few of my past dealings with spirits, and considers himself THE Sherlock Holmes, although we all know he's not. He's sweet on my guardian angel and I like him, even if she seems to find him annoying. Maybe I can get his help, since she's refusing to offer hers.

"Tell me about your day," I say, wanting to be supportive.

"The Gullen land has to be cleaned up." His eyes are steady on mine. "The EPA testing shows it's contaminated with several kinds of toxic metals from when the metalworks plant was in use. They'll be shutting down The Thorny Toad by the end of the week."

Brax and Rhys will be devastated. I'm devastated for them. The business isn't their only livelihood, but it's certainly a big chunk of it. "Have you told them?"

He shakes his head. "One of the reasons I'm late is because I rushed through filing a petition to delay the shutdown. They're using city water, so that's safe, and the building itself passed an air quality inspection last year. There's no reason to put them out of business on short notice. The state should give them at least thirty days."

"Do you think they will?"

He shrugs. "I'll do everything I can to help them."

I pat his hand. "You're a good man."

"I figured it might be easier if the two of us break the news, rather than an officer of the court showing up with an injunction."

"It's Monday night, so the place is closed. I'll text Brax and see if they want to come over and join us for a late dinner."

"I'm really sorry. I know that place is special to you, too."

Aunt Willa did readings there when Brax and Rhys created a hangout for psychics and others with unusual talents. That's one area I haven't followed in her footsteps, but I do kind of like the bar. Daddy occasionally does a live show, and the atmosphere is fun and upbeat. You always feel good when you walk out, even if you haven't enjoyed the libations. "Well, we'll have to find them a different spot to rent."

"There's the old mini-mall off the highway southeast of town."

I grab a sheet of paper, a pen, and my phone. "Let's make a list. It's always best to give a dose of hope when delivering bad news."

Logan smiles at me. "You're a good woman, Ava Fantome." He leans across the table and kisses my forehead. "And I'm glad you're all mine."

＊ 9 ＊

B rax and Rhys take the news the way I anticipated. Brax is a businessman and learned strategic thinking from his mother. Rhys is a bit more emotional and needs a lot of support.

Before they arrive, I pull out the strong liquor. When Brax sees the bottle of whiskey on the table, he knows something big is up. Rhys accepts the food and goes on and on about the day's events, before Brax finally looks me in the eye and asks why I have Aunt Willa's favorite liquor ready and waiting.

I let Logan take the lead and explain everything in detail. Rhys wrings his hands and downs several shots before he claims, "I'm all right." He promptly turns to Brax and follows that up with, "What are we going to do?"

"Don't panic," Brax tells him, taking his hands in his. "We're at a crossroads, but we'll figure it out."

I show them the properties currently for rent. "I'll call Marla Crimshaw first thing in the morning and get her advice," I offer.

She's the top realtor in the area and knows everyone and everything. Brax nods. "We appreciate it. The thing we'll need the most help with is the move. The bar alone will take five or six men. Strong ones. Then there's all the appliances, the inventory, the tables and chairs..."

"The water fountain," Rhys adds.

"We'll be there, and I'll find others," Logan says.

Brax thanks him, even though we all know Logan is up to his eyeballs in work.

Logan offers to help clean up after they leave, but I shoo him off. "Go get some rest," I tell him. "I'll talk to you tomorrow."

While I'm washing dishes, I call my friend who is also a medium. It's ten here, but Winter and her family are on the West Coast. "How are things with the sexy lawyer?" she asks as a greeting.

"He's so busy with work I hardly see him these days."

The sounds of her sisters talking and laughing in the background make me smile. They're all bona fide witches and run a metaphysical shop together. "Set a date yet?"

I rinse a bowl and stack it in the drainer. "Looks like this fall. His mother is pushing for October, after the final grape harvest and while the valley is showing good color."

"Is that what you want?"

"At this point, I'd take five minutes in front of a judge."

She chuckles, and her boyfriend barges in. "Hi, Ava!"

"Hi, Ronan. How are things?"

"Better put Winter on your schedule. She's going to need a dress soon—*eep!*"

A scuffle takes place, filled with mock screams and hooting, before she comes back on the line. "Now, where were we?"

I scrub the soup pot, half-wishing I was there. "Tell me you didn't turn him into a toad or something."

My witchy friend scoffs, but her voice is laced with the sound only true love can produce. "That's too good for that man. When I catch him, I'm reducing him to a slug."

"So, you guys are talking about getting hitched?"

"*He* is. I have other weddings to worry about first."

Her three sisters are all in serious relationships, too. Winter is the eldest and feels somewhat responsible for them since their mother died a while back. "I'm available if you need anything, for you or them."

She thanks me and asks after my folks and my dress line. I bring her up to speed as I finish the dishes. Drying my hands, I lean against the counter and get to the reason for my call. "I have a ghost problem. Two, actually."

"Sounds intriguing." She's moved away from her sisters and the background noise has disappeared. "What's up?"

She loves a good story as much as I do, so I start at the beginning with Reverend Stout's hitchhiker and his unusual behavior. "I need to get that spirit detached from him."

"I've never dealt with possession, but I'm sure I can find info on how to sever that cord. What else?"

"Can a ghost have amnesia?" I tell her about the time capsule and end with my confrontation with Samuel—or whoever he is—in the homestead. "Is it possible?"

"Persephone is crafty, but she can't outright lie. If she believes he's your grandfather, he is. I've never encountered a spirit who didn't know their own identity, but I've learned over the years with magick, and when dealing with earthbound spirits, that almost anything can happen."

"Daddy said the skull had a crack. Do you think a hit on the head messed up his memory in life and that transferred over when he died?"

"Hmm." I hear the squeak of bedsprings and imagine her lying down in her room, away from Ronan and the rest of the family. "Never heard of anything like that, but once again, I guess it's plausible."

"Is there any way to help him get it back?"

She sighs. "Best to just cross him over. The afterlife should return him to decent health, including his powers of recall."

Tabby comes through the doggie door and cries at me. I stick my tongue out at her, assuming she wants to be fed after her disappearing act. She can wait until I'm done talking to Winter. "I have to find him first. One more thing. Could the item he was searching for be binding him here? Persephone said it's his bones, but I wonder if it's something more."

Arthur and Lancelot zoom in at the sound of Tabby's cry. They figure they might get a second dinner if she's fed. Arthur tries to rub against her and she hisses, and I notice she's dirty and looks wet.

"Sure could. Or anything in that box, such as the knife, if it belonged to him. Can you get a better look at it? Send me some pictures?"

A glance outside shows me it's sprinkling. Overhead, I hear the soft rumble of thunder. "Daddy hopes to help with the investigation, so he can probably get me in to examine it. Do you think Redemption might have used it to bind him to the earthly plane?"

"Certain blood hexes can be used for that sort of thing. There may be an inscription or sigil on the handle, so check for that."

Tabby sits at my feet and claws at me. I brush her away. "If that's what it is, how do I break it?"

"Let me do some research. Blood magick isn't my area of expertise, and it's nasty stuff. I recommend contacting those gals who helped you with Logan's family curse. They seem knowledgeable and you're going to need a specialist."

"I thought this was all over—her curse, I mean."

Persephone pops in, waving frantically at me. Her orange hair is on top of her head with a red bandanna and her dress resembles a giant triangle scarf.

What? I mouth.

"You need to get to City Hall," she says. Her eyes are dead serious and my stomach squirms.

"Hold on," I tell Winter. "Why?" I ask the angel.

Tabby races back outside. Arthur and Lancelot look from the swinging doggie door to me.

"Someone's at the dig site." Persephone's face is set with apprehension. "This isn't good."

"Is it Samuel?"

She shakes her head and floats to the main area.

"I gotta let you go," I tell my friend. "Something's come up."

"Call me later when you find out about the knife."

"I will. Thanks." I hang up and follow after Persephone.

She hovers next to my coat where it hangs on a hook by the door. "Hurry," she says. "You have to get there."

I shove my feet into my shoes and grab the raincoat. "What's going on?"

"They're trying to steal the bones."

＊ 10 ＊

Good thing I skipped the alcohol. For a brief moment, I hesitate, glancing toward Logan's place. All the lights are off and I hope he's already in bed.

Inside the car, I wipe my wet face and text my father. The message is slightly cryptic, but he doesn't ask questions about why I want him to meet me at the dig site, pronto.

Rain slashes the windshield as I race to Main Street. Streetlights reflect in the puddles up and down the road and sidewalks. "Persephone," I say with all the warning I can muster. "What am I heading into? Who's stealing them?"

She pops into the passenger seat, nice and dry. "I'm not sure, only that the officer who's supposed to be guarding them is in the building watching ESPN in the administrator's office."

I push the defrost button and wipe at the steam accumulating on the glass with my coat sleeve. "Why would anyone do such a thing?"

"I don't know," she says, voice grim. "But if they take them, you won't be able to break the curse."

"About that." My beams flash across the lot when I turn in, spotlighting a lone squad car. The cop, like she said, must be inside. "Are you sure they're tied to Samuel? He kept going on and on about an item at the homestead he could sense. Maybe that's what is tying him here."

Tabby meows from the backseat and I jump so hard I nearly knock my head on the roof. "How did you get here?" Moot question, but it comes out anyway. "If the love of your life is running around with amnesia, now would be the time to shift to human and help me find him."

"Good luck with that," Persephone says. "She's just got him back, she's not going to be interested in having you cross him over."

"Tough." I shut off the engine, grab my flashlight from the glove compartment, and shoot the cat a contemptuous look. "No good comes from spirits hanging around when they need to move on. If you're not careful, I'll find a way to send you to the great beyond."

She peels her lips back in a silent hiss.

Tightening the belt of my coat, I gird my loins, as Mama always says, by telling myself I can handle whatever—whoever— is out there. "Can I get in without the robber seeing me?"

"Door's locked," Persephone informs me. "The squad should fire this guy."

"I'm sure he didn't expect anyone to be out in this weather attempting to steal a dead man's skeleton."

"Still, it's his job."

"Agreed, but some of us are better at our jobs than others." I spear her with a look before I rummage under the seat for my umbrella. "Maybe I should wait until Daddy gets here. He'll know what to do."

"By that time, our culprit will be long gone!"

She's right, but I'm desperate. "I need to get a stun gun or pepper spray. Between ghosts and nasty townsfolk, I'm always ending up in these precarious situations."

"Whatever you do, Ava, don't try to stop him. He could be dangerous."

"Thanks for the pep talk. Did you see a weapon?"

A curl flies free as she shakes her head. "He's wearing a trench coat. Could have multiple ones hidden under that."

"Maybe I can beat on the administrator's window and get the officer to come out."

"All you have to do is ID the thief," she assures me. "Get a peek at his face. That way, if your father doesn't show up in time to stop him, you can tell the police his name or, if you don't know him, describe what he looks like."

Right. If it's a local, I'll know him. "I can do that."

She pats my shoulder, although her hand goes right through me. "Go get him."

Her touch is rare; it sends goosebumps over me. Tabby cries, as if seconding her directive.

Taking a deep breath, I prep my umbrella and venture into the pouring rain.

The universe has a funny sense of humor and lightning flashes behind the building just as I emerge. Thunder cracks on its heels, seeming like the storm is raging directly overhead, and nearly vibrating my body off my feet.

The blast is so loud, I yip and drop the umbrella. I'm soaked in seconds, and the wind blows the red fabric back and forth in an arc through the mud. "Great," I mumble, my wet hands fumbling with the flashlight as I retrieve it.

Mud drips from the fabric, and with the lightning that close, it isn't wise to give it a rod to zap me. I close the umbrella and leave it on the hood of the car before turning on the flashlight.

At the sidewalk, I sweep my beam across the open lawn and over the tree. Maybe the officer inside will see it and join me. The yellow crime scene tape has come loose from one of the stakes and flutters uselessly in the wind. The blue tarp on the ground is folded back from two of its corners, rain pounding on the overturned soil.

Rivulets of orange clay run into the hole. I raise the light and the ray is nearly lost in the torrent, but I notice a figure in black three feet from the shoddy grave, his back to the beech.

He's wearing a wide-brimmed hat, the edges rippling from the gusts. Rain pours off it, forming a curtain around his face. His head is tipped down, hands crossed in front of him. At his feet lies a large, black duffle bag.

I expect him to look up when I shine the spotlight on him. He doesn't and I wipe water from my eyes as I continue forward. "Hello?" I call.

The storm eats up the word. The edges of his raincoat undulate in the breeze, showering water over his shoes, which are sinking into the mud.

He's as still as a monument and something about his posture sets off alarm bells in my mind. Hesitantly, I step off the sidewalk and pick my way around puddles toward the tarp. I try again to rouse him. "Sir? Are you okay?"

Slowly, as if he's in a dream, he raises his head. He's wrapped a scarf around his neck, nearly covering his chin. As his gaze makes contact with mine, I gasp. Could be a trick of the light, but his eyes seem to glow.

My legs tremble. I can, indeed, identify him, but the being in front of me is not the man I've known my whole life. He is something...other. "Reverend? What are you doing out here?"

"I must bless the..."

The rest is lost in a rumble of thunder. The tree branches creak ominously.

I move past the fluttering tape. "Sorry, I didn't catch that. What?"

He stares at the hole. "The soul is lost. I must bless it and bring it comfort."

At that instant, Persephone appears next to me. "Told you that you needed to take care of that hitchhiker spirit. Now he's fully possessed the poor man."

This day just keeps getting better and better. "I thought it was a harmless ghost. All it does is play the organ and cause mischief."

"There is no such thing," she chides.

Water runs into my eyes and I wipe it away, but there's no

keeping up with it. "In case you've forgotten, he wouldn't let me cross the spirit over."

"Yes, well, now you're in a pickle."

I want to throw the flashlight at her. Lot of good that would do. "How do I get that thing out of him?"

"Exorcism isn't my specialty." Her body begins to fade. "Let me get back to you."

"It's a demon?"

"No, nothing that strong." Her voice shimmers off. "Just a ghost."

Reverend Stout snaps his focus to me. "Demon?" He snarls. "Get away from me."

I hold out a hand in a *wait* gesture. "*I'm* not a demon, Reverend. You know me. It's Ava."

The glow goes out of his eyes and he tilts his head slightly as he fixates on my face. "Ava?"

Relieved at the sound of recognition in his voice, I smile. "Yes." I motion at the building. "Let's get out of this storm."

He glances around, seeming to be confused. When his attention lands on the grave, he steps toward it. "I must bless the bones. They're buried on unconsecrated ground."

"How about you do it tomorrow when it's not raining cats and dogs." I point to the structure once more—the nice, warm, dry building. "We can discuss it in there."

Tires crunch on gravel, the sound cutting through the noise from the weather, and I pray it's Daddy coming to the rescue.

Stout's shadowy face frowns. He continues to stare into the hole, which is filling with muddy water. I don't know if the skeleton will be damaged by that after being buried for so many years, but I bet Detective Jones is going to have a cow anyway.

"Ava?" I hear Daddy's voice call and a second wave of relief sweeps through me.

"Over here!"

The reverend hasn't moved, his hat shielding him once more as he bows his head. He begins to pray.

Daddy rushes up to me, glancing at Stout and back. "What the devil is going on?"

"He claims he's blessing the bones." My father's brows rise in question and I shrug. "Something about them being buried on unconsecrated ground."

"And this has to be done tonight?"

I shrug again. "He's got a ghost problem. He's not thinking straight."

The bleep of a police siren alerts us to Jones' arrival. "I called him," Daddy says, hitching his thumb over his shoulder. "What kind of ghost problem?"

The front door of City Hall opens and the officer in charge rushes onto the porch. "Stop! What are you doing there? This is the police. Get away from the area!"

"You're a little late to the party," I holler at him.

Jones and Daddy used to be partners on the force, and they're still good friends. I, however, have a tenuous relationship with the detective. As he barrels up in a bright yellow windbreaker that's sheeting water, and his officer runs down the steps, Stout continues to pray.

Once he's joined us at the tarp, Jones eyes me from under the brim of his wool hat made dark by the rain. We share a begrudging respect for each other, but I have strong reservations about his intentions most of the time. "What are you doing here?"

Not praying over a skeleton, that's for sure. "I don't believe there's anything the detective can do for the Reverend," I say to Daddy, "but he's welcome to try."

The officer arrives, sliding in the mud to a stop next to Jones. His name tag reads Rowlands. "Whatever is going on here, I will take care of it, sir." He puts his hands on his belt, blinking through the shower. "I just went in to use the restroom." His gaze skips over me to Daddy, then to Stout. "What is going on, exactly?"

He's not familiar to me and may be a transplant. I check my

eye roll, attempting to be patient. "Our minister here believes he's blessing the dead man's bones. No harm done." *I hope.* "Once he's completed that task, Daddy and I will take him home. You can all go back to whatever you were doing."

And I can figure out how to get the ghost out of him.

"Reverend Stout," Detective Jones says, "you shouldn't be here."

The man's lips slow and he peers at us from under the brim. "I'm doing the Lord's work."

"You've violated a crime scene and caused possible damage to the remains of the burial site. The Lord's work is most certainly important, and I commend you for it, but so is observing the law."

"You want me to take him to the station?" Rowlands asks.

"Oh, for heaven's sake." I shake the flashlight at him. "He's praying over some bones, which are probably three hundred years old. While he may not have respected this scene according to your rule books, even if there *was* a crime that put that poor soul in the ground, the perpetrator is long dead, just like he is. The reverend doesn't need a lecture at the station about rules and regulations, he needs warm clothes and his bed."

Jones looks slightly surprised at my outburst. Daddy grins. "We'll take him home, Landon. You two can cover up the hole again."

Jones heaves a sigh, his bulky chest rising and falling under his windbreaker. "I don't know, Nash. Seems like the good preacher needs a talking to."

The officer steps forward, blocking my view of Stout. "He violated a crime scene."

"A *possible* one," I correct. "And he's having some mental issues. There was no intent to disturb the skeleton, only a wish to bless the soul."

"That doesn't excuse the fact—"

A bolt of lightning strikes so close, we all duck and bail from the tarp. I drop the light, Daddy throws an arm around my shoulders from our united crouched positions, and I throw my hands over my ears when the crack of thunder rips across the land, as if God himself has joined us.

When we reluctantly stand, Daddy urges me toward the porch. "Get under cover," he yells above my ringing ears.

Steam rises from a spot near the tree. It stands unharmed, but an ugly jagged black mark mars the lawn next to it. The sign previously posted by the time capsule stone has been destroyed, and the duffle bag has burst into flames.

Jones stomps on them, Rowlands looking on with a blank expression. As I hustle to the building, my stomach churns and my body quakes with shock.

I scan the area near the tree, but the rain and darkness are absolute beyond it. I can see little without my flashlight, and I tremble with a new fear.

Reverend Stout is gone.

❧ 11 ❧

The next morning, I yawn as I put an extra scoop of coffee grounds into the machine and turn it on. What little sleep I did get was haunted with dreams of creepy ghosts and lightning strikes.

Daddy and I searched for an hour, along with Detective Jones, for the reverend, and found him curled up in bed at his house. His wife, Caroline, assured us he was simply tired and a bit under the weather. Daddy suggested he see Doc today, but I could see under her polite smile that Caroline bristled at the recommendation. At least Jones didn't arrest him.

Tabby makes an appearance, nestling in between Arthur and Lancelot. Her fur is clean and dry, indicating she stayed inside after we arrived home. "Do me a favor," I plead with her as the coffee brews, "and find your husband for me. We need to cross him over, Tabitha."

She ignores me, cleaning her ears in the front window once she's finished eating. I take my mug upstairs to shower.

As per our new routine, Logan drops Moxley off after his morning run. He kisses me and rubs my back. "Some storm last night, huh? Did you get any sleep?"

"I almost got hit by lightning," I say with fake brightness.

He sets me from him, his startled expression mixed with concern. "You were out in that?"

"Not by choice. Reverend Stout's ghost may be sort of... possessing him. His erratic behavior yesterday intensified, and I think it's due to his visitor. He decided the skeleton needed blessing, and he went to the site during the storm to pray over it."

"That's crazy." Logan's cornflower blue eyes flash with uneasiness. "Is there anything you can do for him?"

My shoulders feel even heavier with the weight of this new responsibility. "I'm not sure. I have to do some research."

He tugs me to him for a long hug. "I can't believe you almost got hit by lightning. I'm so glad you're okay."

We stay like that for several minutes and I soak up his heat and solidness. After my foray in the rain, I felt like I'd never get warm again.

In the kitchen, he fills his travel mug and I reheat two biscuits for him. He slathers them with butter and leaves after another kiss. I grab one for my own breakfast, adding a bit of Aunt Willa's strawberry jam. I'm on the last jar of it, and it's bittersweet to use it up, knowing she's not here to make more. Strawberry season is almost here, though, and I may try my hand at replicating her recipe.

Moxley and I walk to the back porch as I enjoy my breakfast. Normally, I spend a few minutes out here before the rush of the day begins, but this morning, I have too much to do. I can't relax, so I head down to the homestead, searching for Samuel.

Moxley sniffs around as I amble through the various rooms, calling for my grandfather. I feel a cool chill, but can't be sure it's not simply the early morning air. There are no signs of him, and I don't know where else to look, outside of the cemetery where he's supposedly buried. I've learned that while Hollywood likes to portray spirits haunting graveyards, very few actually hang around there. I don't blame them—what a depressing place to stay. They are, however, often attached to their death site or a loved one. Occasionally, they even anchor to an object.

I study the bedroom fireplace, thinking about what Samuel said he felt. An item. Is he attached to one hidden in it somewhere?

The house smells musty from the rain, the stones in the hearth damp from it seeping through the chimney's cracks. I notice a faded mark engraved in the mantel, but don't recognize it. I brave the cobwebs—and who knows what else hiding in the dark crevices—to run my hand around the interior behind the mantle.

Grimacing at the slimy texture created by a mixture of soot and moisture, I wish I'd brought the flashlight for this inspection. My fingers come away dirty and wrapped in gossamer threads centuries of spiders have left behind. The shell of a dead water beetle sticks to my wrist, entangled in the net.

Entangled is a good word for the predicament Redemption still has my family in. I'd assumed I broke her curse at Halloween last year. Maybe that was only part of it.

After cleaning off the webs and soot, I call Moxley and we head home. I have another ghost to worry about today.

I find Rhys waiting for us on the back porch. The dark shadows under his eyes tell me he didn't sleep. "What are we going to do?" he asks softly as I greet him.

"Come inside and have some coffee." I guide him through the door.

"Brax is so confident, so upbeat about all of this." He drops like a rock into the same kitchen chair he sat in last night. "I'm trying to keep a brave face, but I'm a hot mess."

I pour him a cup and set it in front of him. It's nearly nine and I wanted to check on the ivory dress for Mama before my first appointment. My friend's distress, however, is the most important thing for me to deal with at the moment. "It's perfectly acceptable to be. Brax is, too, under that tough guy exterior. He doesn't want to show it because he knows how upset you are."

Rhys toys with the mug. "He's always my rock."

I grab Mama's favorite creamer from the fridge and hand it to him with a spoon. "He's been mine many times."

"Really?" His coffee turns a buff color as he stirs. "You always seem so...I don't know, strong. Confident. Like Brax."

"Have you met the woman who raised me? We never show weakness. Kiss of death."

He gives me a wan smile and sips his drink. "I put so many hours into the Toad. It was my dream, you know? How can they just shut us down with no warning?"

I take the seat across from him. "It stinks, for sure, but there's not much we can do about that right now. Logan is doing his best to get that thirty-day grace period for you, but whether he's successful or not, we have to prepare for a move."

He rubs his eyes. "I can't even wrap my mind around starting over somewhere else."

"Focus on the upside. You can create a new Toad that's even better." From the kitchen junk drawer, I grab a pad of paper and a pencil. "Let's make a list of all the things you want in it, okay? This will give Marla a starting point for the search."

"What if there isn't any available place, though?"

"Think positive." I create two columns and underline each. "What are your must-haves?"

This gets him thinking, and I write down everything he comes up with. The checklist grows as he embarks on his fantasy bar and grill. A few of the entries I add under the Wish column, rather than Need. Within minutes, we have the page filled.

It's a lot for the realtor to find in one location, but Rhys is out of his fear funk and dreaming about how cool the new space will be. By the time I see him off, there's a spring in his step. Hopefully, my confidence has rubbed off on him.

I call Marla and explain the situation. She commiserates. "That's just terrible. Those poor guys. I'll get right on this and contact you with the best prospects. Off the top of my head, I think the old mini-mall on the highway might be ideal. There were originally three businesses inside it, but the guys can get the whole thing for a song, and knock down a wall to combine two of them. There's lots of light and plenty of storage area."

Both are on Rhys' list. "I'll fax you the list of wants. Warning, it's extensive. We all know you can't get everything on it, but I've put an X by the most important ones."

Rosie and Jenn arrive, chatting away about baby things.

"Perfect. Send it over, and tell Rhys not to worry. I'm on it."

We say our goodbyes and the women wave at me as they hang up jackets and finish their conversation.

"Good morning," I greet them, checking my watch. Our first appointment should arrive in fifteen minutes. "I need to run upstairs and check on something. I'll be right back."

Rosie eyes me as I pass her desk. "I heard you were messing with the skeleton last night."

Someone—probably Officer Rowlands—has been gossiping. "Long story. I'll tell you about it over lunch."

In one of the spare rooms, I flick through the samples stored there. We also keep an assortment of other wedding attire we use as props for the front display windows, along with items we rent to clients for varying occasions. The ivory dress is beautiful, sleek, and at least a size too small for Mama.

I huff. Gloria might be able to adjust it to fit her, but there's no way I can with my limited skills. I'll end up destroying the poor thing, and that won't help anyone.

On my way downstairs, I grab the laundry hamper. My damp clothes are still in it. Carrying them to the utility room, I find Jenn going through several boxes.

"Brought these down from upstairs yesterday, and never got to look through them," she tells me. One's labeled 'bows' and another 'candelabras.' "I thought I could recycle a few things for the wedding on Saturday." She hoists a white satin ribbon in the air and examines it. "Since we don't have time to order decorations, these might be my only choice."

I shove the clothes in the washing machine and add the detergent. "What time are you thinking about holding the ceremony?"

"We want to have a short honeymoon. Nothing extravagant, of course, but I booked two nights in Atlanta at The Whitely for us. It's one of TripIt's top ten hotels." She's gushing again, the ribbon forgotten as she pictures this weekend. "So I'd like to do it in the morning, if that's okay with you."

"That's actually perfect. Ten?"

She bounces a little, despite her belly. "Yes! Oh my heavens, I can't wait."

"You're going to be a beautiful bride." I shut the lid on the washer and heft one of the boxes. "But no more carrying heavy stuff, okay?"

She nods and follows me out. "I thought I'd borrow some folding chairs from the church. There will only be about a dozen of us, and I can hang bows on the backs to dress them up."

Probably best not to bother the minister with that request. "We have white folding chairs at the storage unit. We'll use those. But again, you're not carrying anything. Rosie, either. Recruit someone else to help."

"I can help." Bis is standing near Rosie's desk. She's gotten him a glass of tea and Fern is sniffing at the hems of his pants.

"Awesome," Jenn says. "Penn and BJ will pitch in, too."

"Did the permits come through already?" I ask.

He shakes his head. "The county moves pretty slow with that stuff. I thought I could help locate that item you were looking for yesterday."

He winks.

Did he overhear my conversation with Samuel? "Okay." I don't know what to say, but hey, I'll take all the help I can get. I set the box on the other side of Rosie's desk and Jenn dives in again. Rosie eyes me with a curious lift of a brow. I brush my hands off. "How about I walk you down to the homestead and we can talk?"

He lifts his glass. "Lead the way."

"Tami Jeeves will be here any minute," Rosie reminds me.

"This won't take long." Moxley heaves himself from his bed and follows. He's always up for an adventure, his sharp nose in constant need of a hit off the grass, plants, and trees. "So you can see ghosts as well?" I ask once we're outside. I figure we might as well get right to the point.

"Sort of. I feel them, mostly, but some I can hear." He motions at his gut. "They make my stomach tense up and my ears buzz."

Interesting. "And you can't talk about it to your dad?"

"Absolutely not. When I was a kid and said anything about my imaginary friends, he freaked out big time. Even now, he's squeamish if he hears about ghosts or hauntings. Took quite a bit of persuasion for him to agree to this project. If I were you, I'd hold your conversations with the dead as far from him as possible."

"Noted. Have you spoken to anyone else about your gift?"

"Who am I going to discuss this with? It's not a manly kind of thing, and I can't seem to keep a steady girlfriend. It's hard to focus on one when I feel spirits everywhere I go, you know? They're even in my dreams."

We arrive at the bottom of the hill, the creek's soft rush a background noise to the chirping birds. "Sounds like you need to learn how to set boundaries with them and figure out how to protect yourself. If you want to be a medium and help them, that's one thing. If you don't, you'll need to be able to shut off this gift. Otherwise, they'll drive you batty."

He chuckles as we enter. "Think I'm already losing it."

I understand, but I still ask. "Why is that?"

He shakes his head as if it's too insane to say out loud.

"It's okay," I assure him, "I've experienced some whoppers. Nothing will shock me."

He scratches his head and rubs a hand over the back of his neck. Finally, he concedes. "Yesterday? When I heard that guy talking to you?"

"Samuel. He's my grandfather about eleven generations back."

"The town founder?"

"The very one."

A nod. "Well, when I came downstairs to ask about the original structure, I thought I saw…"

"What?"

He laughs again under his breath. "This sounds like I've lost my mind, but it was a woman. She was watching the two of you from the doorway. She was…wow." His eyes round with awe. "She seemed so real, not ghost-like, you know? Flesh and blood, and I do mean flesh. She didn't have a stitch of clothing on."

Tabitha. "Let me guess, she turned into a cat when she saw you."

His eyes light up and he smiles for real this time. "You saw her, too?"

I pat his shoulder. "I'm quite familiar with her, and believe me, she may be beautiful, but she's also trouble."

At that, Moxley gives a woof, as if whole-heartedly agreeing.

❧ 12 ❧

Our nine o'clock consult is in the chair across from me when Bis returns half an hour later. He shakes his head to let me know he found nothing, and tells me he has to get to work.

"Can we talk again?" he asks, pausing with a glance at Tami, "about the...bananas?"

Code word for ghosts, I guess. "Um, sure. Anytime."

After Tami is gone, I fill in Rosie and Jenn about the previous night's activities, both sitting in stunned silence as I describe our minister's words and actions.

"Poor Reverend Stout," Rosie says.

"You nearly got struck by lightning?" This seems exciting to Jenn. "That's so cool."

"Cool, that's me," I jest. "*I* might be a ghost today if that had happened."

"You've already died a couple times, haven't you?" she inquires. "That's what Penn told me."

"Apparently, I did," I admit. Lucky for me, Logan was there for both experiences and brought me back from death's door. "But I'd prefer we don't broadcast that to the whole town."

Rosie snickers. "Like you can keep anything a secret in this place."

Winter calls, and I send the two of them back to work. Hopefully, she's got info for me. "Exorcising a ghost from someone is not much different than doing so for a demon," she states matter-of-factly. "You're sure it's a ghost, right?"

Versus a demon? I shudder, looking out one of the front windows. "I'm not all that thrilled about working with the dead," I tell her, "so if it's anything beyond that, I'm out. That's not territory I will venture into."

The cats are lying in the displays, enjoying fat rays of sunshine. Persephone appears, sitting in the rocking chair next to the fake fireplace in the exhibit. She fingers the dress on the mannequin wearing my Bellamy gown. "It's a ghost. His name's Marvin Goodwin, and he used to be a Methodist preacher, too."

Now she tells me. "Hold on," I say to Winter, putting her on speaker. "Persephone's gracing me with her presence."

My angel rolls her eyes. "Don't be rude. It's unbecoming."

Mama would agree. "What does he want with Stout?" I ask her.

"Marvin had a thriving congregation in this county. He traveled around to all the small towns and his followers were quite devout. Stout's great-grandpa, Smith, moved to the area during a tent revival tour, and suddenly, he started gaining in popularity. Pretty soon, he was preaching at the Nottingham Hotel and drawing large crowds every Saturday night."

Revenge. A lot of spirits hang around for it. "How did Marvin get stuck at the hotel?"

"He tried to kill Smith and ended up falling on his own knife blade when Smith fought back."

"Are you getting all this?" I ask Winter.

"Loud and clear." I inherited Persephone from her, and she can see and hear the angel like I can. "He wants to torment your preacher and drive him mad."

Or possibly get him arrested. Either way, the reverend will

lose his current congregation. "Please tell me exorcising a ghost is super easy."

Winter makes a hesitant noise in her throat. "Sorry. These things never are, but I'm positive you can handle it."

I wish I had her confidence. "Persephone will be of vital assistance," I say, eyeing the angel. "That's for sure."

She narrows her eyes at me and the orange curls she's stacked high on her head quiver.

"You'll need a cross made of iron," Winter tells me. "Also, Summer says to pick up a couple pieces of black kyanite, if you don't already have some."

I consider my aunt's supply of weird and wacky items in an upstairs trunk. I wouldn't know one black stone from another, although there are a few glassy looking ones. "I think I have obsidian. Would that work?"

"Not the same energetic properties. Black kyanite comes in blade form, and looks like an angel wing. It's a strong aid in channeling spirits, but also highly protective. When you chase Marvin out of the preacher's body, he may try to enter yours. The crystal will keep him out."

Sounded like I needed a bushel of it. "Can I put it on Reverend Stout and do it with that?"

"No, that's what the cross is for. I'm emailing you the rest of the ingredients and directions for the spell I found," she continues. "Let me know if you have questions, and if you're at all unsure of performing this, I suggest having Sage help you."

"You're a lifesaver." *Literally.* What would I do without her? I cross my fingers that Sage will be up for guiding me, too. "I hope you'll let me design your wedding gown. You know, I do have a version named for you."

"It's pretty, but I don't feel like the Snow White type, you know? Not sure what kind of bride I am yet, to be honest. No lace, though, okay?"

I smile. "Making a note now."

After we say our goodbyes, I question Persephone. Ghosts

hate iron and will run from it. "Where can I find an iron cross?"

Her ethereal form moves with the rocking chair even though it appears she's hovering slightly above it. "That's not what you really want to ask me."

I want to quiz her about a lot of things, including where Sherlock is and why was she keeping me in the dark about Marvin? I've long since learned most of my questions won't be answered. No use wasting my breath. "My next appointment is due in five minutes." I wiggle my fingers in a *give it to me* motion. "Cross. Where do I find one?"

She fiddles with the garment again, her hand passing through it as well as the model. "How should I know? I'm not the World Wide Web."

"You're better." Flattery usually helps. "You're tied to this world and the one beyond. Tap into that spiritual internet mojo of yours and help me out."

She feigns boredom, but I know she likes my adoration. "You could try the Historical Society, or perhaps the reverend himself. Even the hotel has a bunch of old crosses lying around."

"It needs to be made from iron."

One shoulder shrugs. "You need a specialty shop, then."

Chicks With Gifts Emporium.

This is what my guardian angel/pain in my backside does— she gives me hints, rather than straight pieces of information. While I appreciate what she does offer, it gets old having to ask her for everything and interpret the clues. "Thank you," I say, begrudgingly.

My email icon lights up with a notification. I scan the information from Winter as I sit.

"Having fun?" Rosie asks from across the room.

My stomach flip-flops at the *Dissolving A Cord To A Ghost* directions. A bath with salted holy water made from the iron cross? "Not exactly."

But if this is what I have to do to restore Stout to his senses, I'll bite the bullet and figure out a way.

First, I need to protect myself. I may be able to accomplish that and locate the cross with a phone call. I scroll through my contacts and find Sage, but before I can dial, I get a text from Daddy.

Exhumation starts in twenty minutes. You coming?

For once, I'm thankful I have a full day. *Sorry, can't. I'm with a client*, I fudge. *Let me know what they discover.*

It's not a lie. We really do have another consult in mere minutes. However, it would be good to have some eyes there, in case Samuel shows up. I find the card Bis left with his personal number on it. He picks up on the first ring.

"I know this is an odd invitation," I say.

"The best kind."

"You don't even know what I'm going to ask."

He chuckles. "I'm working on a leak at the Historical Society. Louise found it when she opened at noon. The storm blew rain under some loose shingles and it's a mess, so she's up in arms because they're having a mystery dinner here tomorrow night with that Butterfinger dude. I assume you're calling about bananas, which is a whole lot more fun."

Weirdo. His reference to the author makes me smile, though. I bet Bis and Daddy would get along great. "In my experience, ghosts—bananas—are the opposite of fun, and the man's name is Butterfield."

"Butterfinger sounds more amusing, and you've been hanging out with the wrong bananas, I guess."

Like I have a choice which kind show up? "If there are fun ones, I'd like to meet them." Although Sherlock isn't bad. "Listen, there's a county forensics expert excavating the skeleton found under the time capsule." Before I can finish, Olivia Montgomery and her mother arrive, bringing in fresh air and excitement. "I'm wondering if our, uh, banana founder might make an appearance." That doesn't sound too strange, does it? "I have a previous engagement, however. Could you possibly bop over and see?"

Rosie greets the mother and daughter team and offers them a refreshment. Mrs. Montgomery accepts, and the two head to the kitchen. Olivia drops into the client chair and flashes me a picture of one of my dresses on her phone. She's grinning from ear to ear.

"Awesome," Bis replies. "What do I do if he is?"

Good question. I give my bride-to-be a thumbs-up. "Tell him I need to talk to him and send him back here if you can."

"Got it. I'll get over there as soon as I can. Time for a lunch break, anyway."

We disconnect, and Olivia launches into what she wants for her wedding. Her mother and Rosie join us, and after the initial discussion about the size of the holiday event and general theme, I excuse myself and let Rosie handle the details.

Moxley follows me upstairs, where I call Sage at Chicks With Gifts. Raven answers, and tells me her sister is out at the moment but will return shortly. I briefly explain what's going on and what I have to do to save the reverend, while Moxley sniffs at the chest in the guest room. "Do you have either item?"

"Hmm. The kyanite is no problem. We always keep a bin of those. Every magic practitioner, psychic, and medium should have a stash. I use mine like a broom at the end of each day to sweep away negative energies that may have collected in my aura. You really should, too, Ava." I hear her moving around and rustling boxes. "I think we have a cross made from some old industrial scrap metal. Could be iron."

My hopes soar. "Can you check?"

"Sure." There's more background noise, some clanging, and finally, a huff from her. "Here it is. Looks like iron to me. It's stamped Gullen Industries."

What are the odds? "It's from the old metalworks building. That's perfect."

"I'll save it for you, and a couple of blades. When do you want to pick them up?"

That's a problem, considering I have no time and they're

twenty minutes or more away. "Not sure. I'll have to rearrange my schedule, I guess. Can I call you when I figure it out?"

I hear the bell at their shop ding. "Here's Sage. Maybe she can deliver."

Another lifesaver. "That would be excellent if she can, but I know you're busy as well." Moxley sits at my feet and stares at me with his baleful eyes, as the sisters talk. I reach down and scratch between his ears, metaphorically crossing my fingers.

Sage comes on the line. "Heard about the excitement. I'm interested in those old bones. I can run your order over to you. Do you think you can hook me up so I can see them?"

Speaking of weirdos. "My dad is helping with the investigation. I'm sure I can work out something. Do I want to know why you're interested in them?"

"Probably not."

At least she's honest. "They're exhuming them now. You might want to come as soon as you can."

"Awesome. On my way."

"Keep an eye out for a slender guy in overalls. His name is Bis. He's a medium." Matchmaking isn't my talent, but hey, what can it hurt to throw them together? "Tell him I sent you and that you know about bananas and are cool with them. I'll catch up with you once I'm done with my current appointment."

"Bananas?"

"Code word for ghosts."

"Gotcha. I like pie," she says, without any segue, "and I hear you're in good with that Queenie chick at the diner."

Bribery at its finest. "'That Queenie *chick* will set your behind on fire for calling her that. She's an awesome baker, and yes, I know her well. I'll buy you every pie in the place if you bring me the cross and kyanite."

"Deal."

Relieved, I say goodbye, round up Moxley, and head downstairs to finish with the Montgomerys.

13

I arrive at the Beehive Diner before Sage. Queenie's lunch rush is still in full-swing, out-of-town faces filling the booths.

WRTV Channel 5's news van is outside and a couple huddle in a corner. I recognize the woman as an anchor who did Mama's interview. Other tourists, either here for the Founder's Week events, or plain nosiness over the skeleton and knife, occupy most of the other seating areas, with the exception of Louise and her companion, Amos Butterfield.

She's laughing and gesturing, telling a story that the author seems to find mildly entertaining. I wonder if he watched the bones being excavated and took notes for his next novel.

Queenie finishes with a patron at the register and waves me over. "All this *Law & Order* stuff if good for business, if nothing else." She motions at the counter. "You here for the special?"

I'm starving but I don't have time for a meal. "Just an iced tea, please. I'm meeting a friend."

She hustles off to get the drink as I take a bar seat. I swivel on the stool, just like I did growing up, and answer a text from Rosie about tomorrow's fittings.

Wednesday is when we showcase my line of dresses, take orders, and work with Gloria to make sure they're a perfect fit for our brides. We've found it easier to set aside one day each week to concentrate on those, rather than to have showings and fittings sprinkled in between our other appointments.

Buster arrives to pick up his lunch order, and Queenie slides the tea in front of me, telling him she's got it ready. He speaks to me and we discuss the weather before she returns with a white bag in hand.

After paying, he bids us both good day and turns to leave. His gaze lands on Louise and he stops at the booth.

The noise in the diner drowns out what he says, but before I swing back to Queenie, I catch sight of Louise flushing and her previous good mood dissolving.

"Your Mama said she's renewing her vows Saturday night." Queenie wipes the counter with a wet towel. "Wants me to stand up with her. I'm too old to be playing matron of honor."

She says it with a note of exasperation, but I know she's pleased. She and Mama have been best friends since childhood. "I didn't realize they were having attendants," I tell her. "But of course, she'd want you next to her."

Queenie smiles. "She's a wonder, your Mama, but she could have told me a little sooner. I have to cater, so I was going to be there in my uniform. For the ceremony, I've got nothing to wear!"

"You could show up in a garbage sack, for all she'd care." I sigh and sip the cool refreshment. "Daddy wants me to give her a gown, but I don't have one that will fit. Not even my ivory sheath dress is the right size, and I don't have time to have Gloria sew an entirely new one. I'd wrap her up like a Grecian goddess, but I'd need her to stand still for longer than five seconds to get the length correct."

Her lips skew to the side as she thinks. "I've got one of those off-the-shoulder puppies. Nothing fancy, but it's lined and a blush shade, very pale. I planned to wear it to a chamber dinner, but it's too small through the bust for me." As is almost everything. The woman is blessed three times over in that area. "I suspect it might fit Dixie, except the length, and I've never worn it. Do you think you could take up the hem an inch or so?"

I grab her arm. "Are you serious? It sounds perfect."

She nods. "I'll drop it by tonight."

All I have to do is figure out how to sew a lined hem. Surely, I can find a YouTube video to walk me through it.

Voices rise behind us. Queenie's gaze flicks to the booth and back. "Those two give me hives with their bickering all the time. I don't know why Buster doesn't just ask her out."

My brows shoot up and I nearly choke on my drink. "On a date? They hate each other."

She stops wiping and gives me a glance that suggests I'm naive. "They've had the hots for one another for years. Drive one another crazy? You bet your beeswax, but that's only because they've never scratched that itch, if you know what I mean."

I feign ignorance. "Why, Miss Queenie, what are you suggesting?"

She grins and snaps the towel at me, then nods at the door. "Your friend is here, or should I say friends?"

I swivel, noting that Louise resembles a tomato that might explode. Sage and Bis enter, and Bis is grinning, Sage appears disinterested in life, as always. She's got a Goth look going on, and lifts her chin in greeting when she spots me.

"The library can wait its turn!" Louise slams a fist down on the table, making her and Butterfield's plates jump. "The Historical Society clearly has jurisdiction over those items, and I will not be pushed around by you or anyone else over this. The time capsule contents are ours!"

Butterfield seems embarrassed, his gaze skimming the audience now watching with rapt attention. Buster sets his jaw for a moment, glaring down at her. "You've made my sister's life hell since you took over the Society, and I won't forget it."

With that, he takes his bag and stomps out, Bis having to step out of his way.

"Back table?" Queenie asks, as if nothing just happened.

I slide off the stool, watching Buster through the window as he gets in his car at the curb and burns rubber backing out and taking off. Candace, on the sidewalk, watches as well, then enters the diner.

Louise is trying not to hyperventilate, and Butterfield has found something on his phone very interesting. Candace strolls by and he does a double-take, watching her as she goes to the counter.

I acknowledge her and nod at Queenie. "Lead the way."

Bis and I seat ourselves at the table, while Sage looks over the glass bakery display. She chews the corner of her bottom lip, and I see she's added a piercing to it.

Bis leans forward and lowers his voice. "She's amazing."

I smile. "She is. Did you see our friend at the exhumation?"

He shakes his head as she joins us, slinging her messenger bag over the chair. "Not a glimpse."

Queenie hands Candace her order, after accepting her payment for lunch. As she leaves, Butterfield once again watches her intently.

Queenie brings us menus, but Bis and Sage don't need them. "I'd like a slice of that chocolate cake," Sage says.

"The Midnight Dream?" Queenie nods. "Good choice."

"I thought you wanted pie," I say.

The girl gives an indifferent shrug. "Changed my mind."

"Water with that?"

"Yes, please," she answers Queenie.

"Would you like anything, Bis?" I ask. "It's on me."

"A Coke would be good," he says. "I already had lunch."

Queenie tucks the menus under her arm and calls a goodbye to some folks on their way out. "You got it."

She walks away and I notice Louise and Butterfield getting up. They've left cash on the table with their bill, and Louise still seems discomfited. He holds the door for her and they part on the sidewalk.

Sage digs in her messenger bag and withdraws a paper sack,

sliding it to me like its contraband. "The stuff you wanted. You probably should let me handle the exorcism, though."

Bis' eyes fly wide. "The what?"

I give him my best fake smile. "Nothing. It's a ghost problem, but I can handle it." *I hope.* "So no sighting of my grandfather?" I confirm. "Were there any other, um, bananas hanging around?"

He shakes his head. Sage glances at the other patrons. "They all know you're a medium. Why are you trying to hide it?"

I lean forward and lower my voice. "For your information, most of these folks are not locals and do *not* know." My gaze lands on the news anchor. "That's the way I prefer to keep it."

"Fine." Another shrug. "If your grandfather is cursed, you'll have to find out how to break it."

She knows what she's talking about when it comes to family curses, and maybe I should rethink having her help me with Stout. "I'm aware, but he's AWOL, and his wife, my cat, won't shift to talk to me."

"I saw her," Bis tells Sage. "She's...wow."

"She's wow, all right." I hold my tongue regarding my frustration with her, even though it's pretty obvious in my voice. "If neither will tell me what's going on, how am I supposed to set Samuel free?"

Queenie arrives with the cake, Coke, and two forks. "In case you two want to share." She winks at Bis and Sage. "Need anything else?"

We shake our heads. "Thank you," I say for all of us.

Bis eyes the huge slice. It's enough for three people. Sage hands him a fork. "You could check the library," she says to me.

I'm confused. "The library?"

She nods and she and Bis both take a bite. "For info on Samuel and his wacky wife's curse."

"I have Tabby's journal. I know why Redemption did it, and I thought I'd broken it, but if I haven't, I'm at a loss. I don't think the library can help with that."

She shakes her head, swallowing a bite of dessert. "The

magickal one. Next to the Emporium. You should call London and have her look up this Redemption gal."

"Magickal library?" Bis' eyes are even wider now. "For real?"

His cell rings, and he checks it. "It's Dad. Gotta get back to work. Miss Louise is stroking about the leak." He looks totally deflated at the thought, but his eyes are earnest when he says, "I'd like to hear more about this place."

"I'll call you," Sage tells him.

Grinning once more, he says goodbye to us and exits.

"Now, the exorcism." She pokes another portion of cake. "It's not something for an inexperienced witch like you to take on."

The tourist in the booth nearby jerks his head toward us, then tells his family they need to go. The two kids aren't even halfway through their chicken nuggets and fries and the girl starts crying.

"I'm not a witch, and please keep your voice down."

She gives me a cheeky smile. "You're awfully tense. You should have a piece of this cake. It's really good."

I watch as the man flips several bills on the table before shoving his wife and kids out the door. I slide the sack from the Emporium into my purse. "If I ate that much sugar in one sitting, I'd be in a coma for days."

The smile widens. "It's better than drinking holy water with salt in it."

I sigh, but have an idea. "My friend said I needed to put him in a bath of that mixture. Do you think simply downing it might work?"

She returns to eating. "Only if the ghost—"

I clear my throat. "Banana."

Her eye roll could take her to the next county. "Only if the *banana* is a lightweight. From the sounds of it, that's doubtful."

"And if we can't get him out with a bath?"

"We're going to need to drown your preacher."

14

My head is spinning as I drive. Sage is a lot more knowledgeable about these things, but I'm not sure how to get Reverend Stout to drink a holy water concoction, much less get him in a tub of it and hold him down until his ghost hitchhiker bails.

After arguing with her for nearly fifteen minutes, I had to leave. She agreed to research and see if she could find a different backup plan, and I shove that away as I beeline for my parents' house. I text Daddy and he tells me neither of them are home, and to go on in. I can sneak in, get the correct length from one of Mama's dresses, and vamoose without her being the wiser.

The place smells of them—not just Mama anymore. Under the coffee and French toast aroma still lingering from their breakfast, I detect individual scents. I stand for a moment and breathe them in—the faintest scent of Daddy's aftershave, her perfume.

She's switched her laundry detergent back to the brand she used when I was a child, I'm guessing because it's his favorite. When my father left, she couldn't stand the memories it evoked and began buying a different one. As I pass the utility room where the washer and dryer are quiet, the fragrance of it hits my nose and makes me halt. A colorful stack of towels rest on top, having been carefully folded, ready to be put away. The scent of the old detergent instantly transports me to my younger years.

I even catch the whiff of guitars and their cases as I move through the downstairs rooms. One of the cases is open in the living room, the instrument inside waiting for him to pick it up and start playing. A mixture of the wood, stain, and lining join together to once more remind me of the past.

Upstairs, I feel out of place entering their bedroom. I've been in here hundreds of times when it was just Mama's. It's good that she's no longer alone, and they're so in love again. As I locate the dark navy dress that's her favorite, I pray Logan and I will be as happy as they are all our lives.

Mama's sewing basket is buried in the hall closet and it takes me a few minutes to locate the measuring tape inside. I hang the red plastic band around my neck like Gloria does and fish out my phone. I not only gauge the length, but also note the dimensions of the chest and waist. Might as well be sure that I can adjust Queenie's garment from top to bottom if necessary.

Back in the car, I race home to find our next appointment waiting. Jenn is chatting with the woman at my desk. Arthur is winding himself around Kitty Buchard's ankles, and she dotes on him. "Who's a good boy?"

Lancelot, not to miss out on the attention, runs in and hops in her lap. Luckily, she's a cat person and thinks it's great. Moxley eyes all of them from the window for a moment, and then flops his head back down to return to his nap.

Rosie looks pale and I check on her before joining them. "Are you okay?" I ask under my breath.

She closes her eyes and rubs her forehead, sinking back in her chair. "All of a sudden, I'm really tired. I probably should have eaten more at lunch."

"Why don't you take off early? I can handle this afternoon."

She blinks her eyes open and shakes her head, sitting up slowly. "I'll be fine."

"Do you want to go upstairs and lie down?"

'Bullheaded' is her middle name, and she insists she will be okay. I drag her from the chair and into the kitchen. "Let's try a bit of food and drink." I get her a cup of tea and make her prop her feet up while I heat a bowl of leftover chicken and dumplings. "Stay here until I get back," I command, placing it in front of her. "No working. Just eat and relax, okay?"

Diving in, she nods. "You're a pretty good cook, you know that?"

"Thanks." I touch her shoulder. "I need you rested and ready for this weekend, so don't be getting sick on me."

She laughs. "I promise, I'll be fit as a pregnant fiddle."

At my desk, I take over from Jenn, but covertly ask her to keep an eye on Rosie. She deftly moves back and forth between her and my office during the course of the next few minutes, bringing me books of samples for the retirement party Kitty's planning for her husband, and making sure Rosie is doing okay.

Usually, I hand the specifics of our event planning to Rosie, but today, I have to fill in all the forms as I walk Kitty through the themes and options. Jenn pipes up when we're discussing the pros and cons of various venues and suggests the new golf gaming place, Summit, eight miles outside of town. Calling themselves an "entertainment destination," they feature dozens of climate-controlled hitting bays with HDTVs, along with a sports bar & restaurant. "They have amazing food," she tells us. "I don't golf, but they have other games and a dance floor. It's super fun."

Kitty's husband is an avid golfer. "He mentioned going there for his birthday. That might be the perfect idea."

I haven't visited yet, but one of their reps recently contacted us about their packages. "They have a roof-top terrace and spaces for private events," I tell her as I bring up their website and turn my laptop so she can click through the pictures and info. "I'm sure he'd get a kick out of being able to golf during or after the actual celebration, and like Jenn mentioned, there are several other types of entertainment for those who don't play."

She loves the suggestion and half an hour later, I've called their coordinator and secured the date. After she leaves, I thank Jenn. "I'm glad you were here to recommend that place."

"Just doing my job," she says with pride in her voice.

"After the baby comes, you should bring him or her here, if you want to continue to work part-time for us."

Her face brightens. "That would be amazing. I will definitely take you up on that. We don't know where Jeremy will be stationed after his promotion is finalized, but I'm hoping we can stay in this area."

Rosie is back, and while she puts on a chipper smile, I can see the strain around her eyes. "You need to go home and rest. Do you want me to drive you?"

Fern peeks out from under the desk, then scurries to her bed. "I'm fine," Rosie insists. "You're fussing like an old hen."

"Is the baby kicking?" Jenn asks.

She nods. "Nonstop last night and today. It's wearing me out."

"She's going to be a sassy one." I grin at her. "You'll have your hands full."

When she won't take the afternoon off, I put her upstairs in the guest bed with her laptop. Jenn brings a pitcher of water and a glass, and we get her propped up and comfortable. "Text if you need anything," Jenn tells her.

In my office, I call Rosie's husband. He's at work, but I want him to know she's off her game. While concerned, he tells me she had this with their son, Matt, too, and he'll leave soon and get her. Neither of us wants her to overdo it.

The rest of the afternoon goes by in a rush. I don't have time to check the rental properties Marla faxed over until after five. I check in with Rosie, who's now home, and she informs me she had a nice nap after her husband insisted she rest, and the baby has settled down.

Jenn leaves with a wave after I'm off the phone. "See you tomorrow. Do you think Gloria will bring my gown?"

I haven't had a chance to check on it, but I have no doubts the seamstress has been hard at work. "Of course. Have a good evening."

"I'm not sure I can sleep. I'm so excited to see it."

After she's gone, I kick off my heels, grab the faxed pages, and take Moxley to the back porch. I need a cup of tea, or better yet, a glass of wine, but I'm too lazy to get either. I let him out the screen door to sniff in the grass, and I check the perimeter for any ghosts. None appear, so I sit and read through the properties.

Two are possibilities, but the other five are disappointing. When my cell rings, I set them aside and smile, seeing it's Logan. "Hey, good lookin'."

"I'm done early and on my way home. Thought I'd pick up some specials from Queenie, unless you cooked."

I haven't even thought of what to make. "Throw in a bottle of wine and I'll be yours forever."

"Deal. See you in a few."

We disconnect and I walk barefoot across the lawn to Brax and Rhys' property. They have several guests for the week at their B&B, including Butterfield. He's on an Adirondack chair in the yard. "Evening," I say as I pass.

He glances up from a book, removing a brown-colored cigarette from the corner of his mouth and nods. "Evening. I don't believe we've officially met."

"Ava," I say, accepting his outstretched hand as he rises. "And you're our famous mystery writer. Getting any good tidbits to throw into your next novel?"

He offers a long-suffering smile, puts out the cigarette, and closes the book. "Inspiration is everywhere."

I bet it is, especially in this town.

"I hear you can talk to ghosts." He states, walking with me to the back door. "I wonder if I could ask you a few questions?"

I stop in mid-step. "Sorry?"

"Your ability as a medium would be a good plot device in my next whodunit. It's important I understand a character thoroughly. I always do in-depth research so the protagonist and his or her nemesis jump off the page to the reader. I want to get under your skin, so to speak."

Not too creepy. "Trust me,"—I resume walking, and speed up—"You do not want to get under *my* skin. I wish you the best with that storyline, but I'm not…" I don't know how to finish. I'm not going to lie about my skills, but I sure as heck don't want to be the model for one of his characters. "Anyway, I just need to drop these off."

He jogs to keep pace with me. "How long have you been a ghost whisperer? They tell me you died and came back to life. What was that like? Is that when it started?"

I burst into Rhys' kitchen and luckily he's at the stove. "Hi, sugar," he says.

"I have lots more questions," Butterfield continues, nearly plowing into my back. "We really must chat."

Seeing my disconcerted expression, Rhys sets down the spoon he's holding and grabs my arm, steering me away from the author. "Tell me you've found a new place for the Toad."

He draws me into the tiny utility room on the side, shutting the door behind us. "Thank you," I say under my breath in case the man is eavesdropping.

"What happened? You look like he threatened your cat."

"It's not important." I hand him the top prospects. "These don't have everything on your wish list, and Marla is still looking, but check out the top two. I think you could turn them into gold. The locations are excellent, the square footage is perfect, and they are both empty, so you could move in right away and begin work."

He accepts the papers and kisses my cheek. "Do you want to stay for dinner? Butterfinger's leaving for a signing at the Historical Society, so he won't bother you."

Now he's calling him by the nickname, too. "I thought it was at the library."

Rhys glances at the pages. "I guess Louise decided to have one at the Society as well. Can't be outdone by BayBay." He uses his nickname for the librarian, and returns his focus to me. "The other guests are quite nice. I think you'll love Janet."

"I wish I could, but Logan's coming with takeout. Raincheck?"

He winks. "Anytime."

Checking the coast is clear, I hurry out and breathe a sigh of relief as I arrive back at my house. Moxley is waiting on the porch steps, his droopy eyes focused on the house down the hill.

"What is it, Mox?" I stare at it as well. "Did you see Samuel?"

He barks and something catches my eye as it passes like a shadow across the upstairs window.

I'm running for the homestead before I can think, Moxley on my heels.

$$\text{\decofourleft}\quad 15 \quad\text{\decofourright}$$

A voice rings out as I draw near. "Tarnation, woman! I am attempting to save your soul!"

The response is a familiar screech by a feline. I'm well acquainted with that sound—it's the cat version of a lion's roar, no less fierce for its more diminutive source.

"Samuel?" I call, rushing inside. "Don't try to—"

He yelps and I cringe, remembering the sensation of her claws raking my skin. Tabby races past and through the door, and Sam floats into the main area, shaking his wounded hand. "You again," he says, flicking a glance my way.

"Good to see you, too. So, she can scratch you?" I stare at his injury in astonishment. "Interesting, since you're a ghost."

"As is she, in certain aspects." He covers the marks with his other hand, pressing on them, but not before I note he's bleeding. It's paler than human blood, much like he's a pale figment of what he was in corporeal form, but it's definitely blood. "She is bound to this land, as am I, and neither of us can leave it. We are cursed."

"But she's a cat, not a ghost, and you're..."

"Dead?" he finishes for me. "Quite so. She relishes her

magick and uses it to look after our progeny, but it is not natural."

"So you remember who you are?"

He scans the walls, glances at the ceiling. "My memory is beginning to return, yet I continue to find myself at a loss on many matters."

"Join the club." Moxley catches up and sniffs the air in Sam's direction. "How exactly do you think you're going to help her?"

"What she did—her magick—has tarnished her soul. I don't believe either of us can move on because of it."

"What exactly did she do?"

"As I have already mentioned, she used magick to tie us to this land. She went a step farther and turned herself into a cat with nine lives so she can watch over our children and grand-children."

She has never struck me as the maternal type, but I have to admit, I don't know her all that well. "Was it some kind of spell?"

He raises a thick brow at me. "Do you know of another way to change into feline form without witchcraft?"

Can't say I do. "She is—was—a white witch. She hasn't harmed anyone. Not like your first wife."

His face goes blank. "I have more than one?"

"Does the name Redemption ring any bells?"

He staggers back, fear replacing the baffled expression, as he glances around furtively. "I remember! Do not say her name!"

A chill sweeps up my spine. Moxley barks and swings around to face the entrance. I glance over my shoulder, hoping to see Tabby, and not Redemption. Neither are there. "Why? She's long dead. Isn't she?"

"Names are powerful. *She* was powerful." He calls her several vile epithets and spits. "That witch nearly killed me."

Nearly? Hmm. "How?"

"She hexed me, and when that didn't work, she..."

"Ava?" I hear Logan's call echo in the backyard.

I walk to the door and holler back. "Be right up!"

When I turn to finish the conversation, however, Samuel is gone.

"Tarnation," I mimic under my breath to Moxley. "That man is annoying."

Inside, Logan is pouring wine and talking on his phone. A garment bag lies across a chair and a big Beehive Diner bag is in the center of the kitchen table.

Moxley greets him with enthusiasm and Logan hands me a glass before bending to make over him. "Mother, Saturday night is the Fantome party." He stands and kisses my cheek as she replies, then rolls his eyes. "I know Chuck hasn't been home since Christmas, but we're already committed. You *are* coming, right?"

He ambles out of the kitchen, tucking the phone between his ear and shoulder so he can roll up his sleeves. I sip the wine, fingers too tight on the glass. Is she trying to usurp my parents' anniversary celebration? Surely, Helen wouldn't stoop so low as to make Logan choose between a dinner with her and this event, would she?

The garment bag holds Queenie's dress. I move it upstairs, then return and busy myself pulling out white containers from the food bag. Looks like her famous ham steak and potatoes were the special tonight. I try not to drool.

Smelling food, the cats race each other into the room, nearly running into Moxley. I leave the takeout covered, not knowing how long Logan's conversation might take, but hoping we don't end up with a cold meal. The irritation burning in my blood might just keep it hot.

I feed the pets and set the table. I hear him in the front room. "The ceremony begins at four. I can come by afterward and hear Chuck's announcement. The Fantomes will be disappointed if you don't show. Ava will be, too."

Charles Cross is Logan's younger brother by two years. He owns a brewery a few towns over and sees fit to stay away from Thornhollow as much as possible. His relationship with his mother is strained because he wouldn't remain with the family business and embarked on his own. She's still peeved at Logan for doing the same, but forgives him because he's still in town. While Chuck is successful, his company is small potatoes compared to the winery.

I wonder what his news might be. A girlfriend? A secret baby? Is he coming out of the closet?

Tabby finishes her meal and begins cleaning her front paws. I sip more wine and eye her, half-listening to Logan, and half-trying to decide how to force her to shapeshift and confess.

Logan returns, running a hand through his hair and making it stand in spikes. "Ava and I are about to have dinner, Mother. I'll talk to you tomorrow."

He ends the call without a goodbye and tosses his cell on the table. I pour him some wine and hand it over. "Sounds like your mother is working that Helen Cross juju on us."

It's my way of criticizing her need to push her weight around without saying she's a you-know-what. Under her tough exterior and the need to rule the roost, I know she's a match for my own mother.

He swirls the liquid. "Chuck has a big announcement and is coming by Saturday night to make it. He wants all of us there for it, so Mom wants to have a formal dinner."

Of course she does. I sit and begin opening the lids on the containers and scooping food onto our plates. "So you can hang out with us for a few hours and then swing by their place."

A heavy sigh and he plops in his chair. "Exactly what I told her."

"But she's still upset."

He points his fork at me. "Bingo."

I love Logan and will do whatever I need to in order to make him happy. His mother, though, is worse than ten Persephones. "Call Chuck and see if you can meet with him beforehand or if he'll come Friday night instead."

Around a mouthful of potatoes, he says, "Good idea. I've always been good at making him talk."

My lawyer. "We'll work it out. Tell me about your day."

As we eat, we catch up, and I almost stop worrying about Reverend Stout, Samuel, and Mama's dress. "Any word on the petition to get Brax and Rhys more time?" I ask.

"Nothing yet, but I called Judge Barlow and asked for him to personally look into it. He owes me a favor, so fingers crossed."

I hold up both hands in a stop gesture. "I'm worried about you. You're working too hard."

"So are you." He polishes off the last of his dinner and wipes his mouth. "How are you going to get the ghost out of our minister? We need him for our wedding, you know."

The weightiness of the situation comes crashing back down on me. I gather the empty plates and take them to the sink. "Water sanctified by a cross made of iron and purified with salt."

He joins me at the sink, rinsing the dishes. "Sounds simple."

I laugh without humor and plug the drain. "If I can't get him to drink the concoction, I have to drown him in it."

"Not literally."

I take the plate he hands me. "Actually, yes."

He turns and grabs my shoulders, making me face him. "You can't be serious. Ava, that's…"

"Crazy? I know, but if the ghost won't come out the easy way, I may have to resort to more intense measures."

"I was going to say, premeditated murder." Releasing me, he shakes his head and mimics blocking his ears. "Don't say anything else about it."

"I'm not going to kill him." *I hope.* I shift the water so it runs into the basin and add soap. "I promise not to implicate you should things go wrong, but really, you should have more faith in me."

"We're not married yet." He refills our glasses with the last of the wine. "They could call me to the stand to testify against you."

I can't tell if he's teasing me or not. I've been trying to ignore the fact this is perilous and I have no business doing any such thing, but I hear a note of sincere concern under his offhanded comments. I pivot and lean back against the counter, my heart dropping to my knees. My stomach clenches around my dinner and it threatens to come back up. "You're right, what am I thinking? This is completely insane."

Sympathy cuts across his features and he pulls me into a hug. "There has to be another way to save him. You'll figure it out."

We're both so tired, we fall asleep on the couch before the ten o'clock news. My phone rouses me when it rings, and I see a familiar number on the screen. Logan, awake now, too, rubs his eyes and stretches. "Who's that?"

"Daddy."

"Better take it." He leans over and kisses me. "We'll see you in the morning."

He and Mox leave as I answer. "Hey. Everything okay?"

"You asleep already, kiddo?"

I yawn. "It's been a rough week and it's only Tuesday."

"I can call you tomorrow."

Shutting off the TV, I blink away the sleep. "It's okay. I'm up now."

"I wanted to tell you about the preliminary report from the forensic anthropologist. He won't give us an official one until he's had time to fully inspect the body, but it looks like our skeleton is pretty old, probably a hundred years or more. Hard to pinpoint it accurately because of the damage done by the soil. But he's sure of a couple things."

Walking around, I turn off lights and head for the stairs. "I'm listening."

"It's a woman, guessing between forty and fifty, and there were extra bones with her."

Tabitha? "What do you mean extra?"

"Small ones. Something was buried with her."

My stomach falls. "A baby?"

"An animal."

I hit the top of the stairs and see the marmalade feline on my bed, curled up and sleeping. "Let me guess, a cat?"

"Could be. The doctor was focused on the woman today. He'll do more evaluating of the other bones once he's done with her."

So it wasn't Samuel, it was Tabby. "Could he tell if she died of natural causes?"

"At this point, no, but even if she was murdered, it was so long ago, there's no chance of discovering the killer."

Exactly as I suspected. That means there's no case. I hear the disappointment in his voice. "Do you think I could examine the knife tomorrow?"

"What for?"

"Curiosity," I tell him, which is true.

"Does this have to do with our vicar's ghost?"

"Not his, but another. I won't touch it or anything, I just want to see it."

"Jones is having the blood on the cloth tested for DNA, but I don't think he'll oppose you getting a look at knife. Louise is already petitioning for it to be at the Society."

"No surprise there, but why would she want it?"

He sighs. "My thoughts exactly. Guess it's a relic from an earlier time period and should be respected as such."

A possible murder weapon on display. Sign me up for that. "Thanks, Daddy. Keep me posted."

"I will," he says. "Get some sleep."

I try, but after an hour of tossing and turning, I finally get up and stare at Queenie's dress. I get comfortable at Aunt Willa's sewing machine and acquaint myself with the various parts. I used it and Mama's a few times growing up, when Home Ec or a summer camp demanded it, but I'm rusty.

Focusing on that and learning how to hem a lining, however, allow my worried brain to relax. Some of my best ideas come when I concentrate on something entirely different.

I find one of Aunt Willa's old outfits to practice on and watch an instructional online video. It seems straight forward.

Attempting to hem the thin lining of my aunt's dress is anything but. The slippery material binds and I realize I have the wrong type of thread. I search through the drawers of the stand and find several rolls of polyester. I pick one, wind a bobbin—no easy task—and try again.

Two hours later, I quit. My stiff neck is killing me, and I'm finally ready for bed. The practice dress is hemmed, though, and for my first attempt is not too bad.

Before I drift off, I call Winter. "I can't kill the preacher," I tell her when she answers.

"*Kill* him? What is going on?" I hear her moving around. "I thought you were cutting the cord to his ghost."

"I now have three spirits, and they all need help." Arthur snuggles close to me, leaving Lancelot next to Tabby at the end of the bed. I spend the next few minutes bringing her up to speed. Like Logan said about the exorcism, I have to find another way. "I think it's Tabitha's skeleton anchoring Samuel here, but regardless of what's going on with the two of them, I have to save Reverend Stout, and I refuse to drown him. There has to be a different option."

"I still think a basic bath will work, but it sounds as if you need the big guns," she states. "Let me call Mama Nightengale and get her input. Don't do anything until I get back to you, okay?"

Mama N is the daughter of a long line of voodoo practitioners who happens to be Winter's neighbor. She knows a lot about hexes and dark magick. "Thank you."

We disconnect, and relieved to know we will figure something else out, I fall asleep.

✽ 16 ✽

Wednesday dawns bright and clear, but my head is killing me.

I slept poorly, dreams of ghosts running from me and zombies rising from the ground to chase after me. Barely functioning when Logan drops off Moxley, I hand him a piece of toast with jam on it—the best I can do for breakfast—and wish him a good day before I jump in the shower.

When I return, I find he's left a steaming cup of coffee outside the bathroom door, and a bowl of fresh fruit waits for me on the kitchen table.

I love this man.

Our first appointment is Lana Sims, who can't decide on a dress. She loves The Bellamy with its simplistic lines and flapper-inspired glitz, but she also feels the same about The Winter. She'll try on samples again, and hopefully, make a decision.

Rosie arrives first, seeming more chipper. "Good morning," she calls out.

From the kitchen, downing more coffee, I reply and drag myself to her desk. I've already replaced The Bellamy sample on the mannequin and have it ready for Lana when she arrives. Winter sent me some info from her voodoo friend and things don't look good. Getting that hitchhiker out of Stout is going to be hair-raising, no two ways around it. I've decided I have to tackle one thing at a time, and right now, I need to make sure Rosie is up to par. "How are you?"

She sets down a travel mug and apple on the desk. Fern hops from the tote and nestles under a blanket in her bed. "Much better. I overdid it yesterday and didn't watch my food intake. Low blood sugar gets me every time. I'm better equipped today."

Jenn comes early, since she loves Wednesdays and watching brides try on the designs and have their fittings. This morning we have Lana and two other 'lookers' as we call them, and hope all three decide to buy.

The afternoon is reserved for fittings with those who've already chosen their gowns. Gloria and her partner, Joseph, take care of the details. Together, they run Miss Jasmine's Boutique Bridal Designs, and thankfully, they've fallen in love with my line, and are putting in the hours to supply all the orders I take.

Lana shows up early, eager to begin. Her maid of honor and mother come with her. Jenn takes her to my uncle's old den, which I've remodeled as a changing room. I left most of his furniture, repainted the forest green walls a pale pink—after multiple coats of primer—and added a screen for privacy. Wedding parties can be with the bride if she wishes, or they can sit in the main area until she comes out for the reveal.

Lana's party waits on the sofa and Rosie offers them tea and coffee. The mother asks after Mama and we discuss the weather, the Founder's Day excitement, and she requests I convince her daughter that The Bellamy is the better choice because it makes her hips appear smaller.

Skirting issues such as this is a full-time job in my line of work. I assure Mrs. Sims that Lana will be breathtaking in either design and ask about her mother-of-the-bride attire.

While she's explaining her color choice, my cell rings. I excuse myself to take the call from Daddy. "I got the okay from Landon. Can you be here at ten?"

"At the station? Sure." If all goes according to plan, Lana will pick a dress before then. "Thank you, Daddy."

When Lana comes out in The Winter, her eyes sparkle with joy. I know her mother doesn't appreciate this dress as much, but Lana's full-figure actually looks amazing in it. I help the bride onto the platform in front of the mirror and fiddle with the modest train, helping Jenn fluff it out. Lana beams. "I feel like I'm in a fairytale."

Her maid of honor looks from her friend's happy face to Mrs. Sims' less than thrilled one. She doesn't want to get in hot water with either of them. "It's beautiful on you," she states.

I puff the short sleeves and eyeball the waistline. "If we take this up an inch, it will give you a bit more train." I lift the fabric, raising the waistline to show her. "You could definitely carry it."

The higher waist camouflages her hips a bit and I notice Mrs. Sims scrutinizing Lana's backside with more interest. "That's preferable," she states.

Lana's face falls. "You don't like this one?"

"I want to see you in the other. It complemented your figure better."

Lana's disappointment is palpable. Releasing the skirt, I choose a veil from the nearby selection. "Before we do that, let's see this one with a few accessories."

I tuck the combs into her hair and Jenn helps me adjust the fine material to spread it over her backside. This headpiece has matching rhinestones and pearls, and puts the finishing touch on the look. Jenn and I select several articles of bling from our loaner collection, including a necklace that spotlights Lana's generous bosom and draws the eye to her face.

"Oh," Lana breathes. "It's so gorgeous. I'm gorgeous." Tears form in her eyes. "I've never felt like that."

Jenn takes several shots with Lana's phone so she can study them later, if she doesn't commit today. Then she walks her to the changing room and I smile at her mother. "She is absolutely stunning in that gown. She lights up in it."

"I know what you're trying to do, Ava Fantome, and I understand you want her to be happy. But ten years from now, she'll look back on her photos and know that I'm right."

"We have hip huggers," Rosie volunteers from her desk. "They minimize and contour, if you want to suggest she try one on."

Personally, I wish every woman would embrace her body, regardless of the shape or size, but I also commiserate with anyone who wishes to accentuate their assets and downplay those that make them feel self-conscious, especially on their wedding day. "If we raise the waistline a half inch, it will deemphasize the hips."

"I think she looks amazing in it, too," the maid of honor adds, gaining courage. "A decade from now, she'll see her pictures and remember how happy she felt, not how big or small her hips were."

Irritation takes root in Mrs. Sims' expression, and hoping to divert a scene, I point at her half-full glass. "How about a refill?"

Like a well-oiled machine, Rosie whisks in and asks about the reception, diverting the conversation like a pro, as I head to the kitchen.

By nine-fifty, Lana has decided on The Winter and all the forms have been completed, her mother reluctantly onboard. The wedding is in August, so there isn't much time to produce the gown, but the church and other items are already arranged, which takes a big load off us.

I'm two minutes late to the station, but Daddy greets me with a hug. "Ready?"

The original police department, established in 1854, was housed near the then railroad tracks. It was hit by a tornado, wiping it out, only to be rebuilt and later destroyed once more during the Civil War. During Reconstruction, the center of town shifted west several blocks and a new station was built. It's been here ever since.

I pull out my phone and hit the camera icon, then follow him to the evidence room. My plan is to be out of here in five minutes and drive to the Magickal Library of Witches and Wizards to have Paris and London help me dig up info on Redemption. "Thanks for doing this."

"Anything for you."

The place smells of old coffee and iron bars. I see a ghost pass across a long hall on my left. It's not Samuel, and seems to be a residual energy left behind by a former inmate. These types of imprints from time and generations of folks living and dying are layered on top of real life everywhere I go. There are true spirits stuck here, and I try to help those I can, but I've learned to ignore most of these residual energies. They aren't ghosts in the full sense of the word, more like loops of time. "Have you and Detective Jones figured out anything more about the skeleton or what the knife was used for?"

"The forensics fellow thinks it may have been a ceremonial blade. The blood on the cloth will tell us more about its final use. He believes the victim died of natural causes, and it appears she broke her leg once. Good teeth, though. He found that unusual, considering the time period he estimates she lived."

We stop outside a door with a frosted glass panel and Daddy unlocks it. Our town is small, and so is its evidence locker. The shelves are full, boxes with dates and record numbers going back before the Civil War. There aren't many from then, as most of those were destroyed, but some survived and continue on in the cool, tiny room.

As Daddy writes his name on the log and sits at the 1990s computer at the desk to fill out the paperwork, I study the rows of cartons. How many people's lives, perpetrated or affected by one crime or another, are detailed here? How many of my relatives?

Daddy finishes and clicks off, swiveling in the squeaky seat. "Okay, it's over here."

One of the newest cardboard boxes sits on the floor, missing the layer of dust prominent on its predecessors and still unfaded by time. Daddy lifts the lid and scoops out the bagged weapon.

The bloody cloth is absent, since they're testing it. I hold it up and observe it in the glare of the overhead fluorescent fixture. "This doesn't look ceremonial. More like a kitchen knife."

"I thought so, too, but I'm no expert."

Although it's Thornhollow, Daddy has seen his share of crime scenes, and I'm pretty sure he knows his weapons. "I'd take your opinion over the expert's any day."

He smiles. "You're biased."

"I most certainly am." I use a thumb to shift the writing on the evidence bag out of the way to examine the handle. There are a series of scratches on it, markings that appear homemade and unrefined. I lay the bag on the desk and reposition it, trying to get a good closeup of them. The one that stands out to me is a match for the fading symbol carved into the fireplace at the homestead. I've never seen any like the rest, but I'm counting on Winter or another of my friends to recognize them.

Daddy eyeballs the handle over my shoulder. "Those what you were looking for?"

"Sure are."

"What do you think they mean?"

I snap a few more pictures then pocket the phone. "No clue, but I'll figure it out. There's a similar one to this"—I point at the design—"on the bedroom fireplace at the Thorn-Holloway home. As I suspected, I believe this knife is linked to Samuel and Tabitha."

Daddy takes the evidence bag and raises his brows. "Do you think the woman from the burial is her?"

"Possibly. The knife may have been hers as well."

He reaches in and pulls out another bag. "That symbol is on this band we found on her left ring finger."

The metal is dull with tarnish. I can still make out two hands holding a heart between them. Was this Tabitha's wedding ring?

Daddy motions for me to examine the interior. I have to

place it, bag and all, under the desk lamp to see more clearly. Without a magnifying glass, it's hard to make out what's etched inside, but there seems to be the same symbol slightly worn with age. This version does have crisper edges and appears as though it was stamped into the metal.

Daddy stares at the matching one on the knife handle. "The top section kind of looks like a flower, doesn't it? Or maybe that's supposed to be a head with a bad hairdo."

I take a photo of the ring, even though I can't get a good shot of the stamp inside. "I'd sure like to know if Tabitha is buried in the cemetery. I know there's a headstone, but who or what is there—if anyone—is up for grabs at this point. Figuring that out could eliminate the possibility she's our Jane Doe."

He returns the knife to the box. "Exhuming a body requires a judge to sign off. I doubt you'll find one who thinks a three hundred year old mystery is worth the time and effort."

I hand him the bag with the ring. "I know it's a long shot, and maybe it *doesn't* matter, but if that skeleton is Tabitha, she deserves to be laid to rest in the churchyard."

He secures the lid. "When did she supposedly pass?"

My memory is bad with dates. "I think 1760-ish. All I remember is that Samuel died the same year."

"So, if she was originally buried in the cemetery, someone dug her up and moved her to the spot under the time capsule."

I raise a finger as an idea hits. "Assuming the capsule was originally buried in that location."

We stare at each other, turning that possibility over. "Thinking like a detective, now, are you?" he asks, grinning.

It all has to be tied to Samuel being stuck in the time capsule, and Tabitha performing magick to steal a cat's body and use its nine lives to keep watch over her descendants.

In the end, does it really matter where she's buried? If I can figure out how to un-anchor Samuel and get him to pass over, that's the important thing. Tabitha will have to work out her soul stuff on her own. "It's a mystery for sure." I kiss his cheek. "I've got to run. Thanks again."

He walks me out, passing the three cells. My nose is hit with the scent of iron, concrete, and sweat. Crime in Thornhollow rarely garners more than a speeding ticket or an overnight stay in one of the cells for those who imbibe too much. More serious criminals are sent to the county jail as soon as possible.

Outside, Daddy holds the car door for me. "Speaking of mysteries, are you attending the dinner tonight?"

"I hadn't planned on it." I get behind the wheel and crank the engine. "Mama making you go?"

His mouth crooks up on one side in a display of capitulation. "She likes that kind of stuff and says it's only right for the mayor to attend and support the Society and the theater actors."

"You'll have the murder figured out before it happens."

This gains me a true smile. "Usually do."

"Which is why I will bet on you and your conclusions any day of the week. See you later."

He shuts the door and waves. As I pass the church and the graveyard behind it, I wonder how I'm going to prove Tabitha's remains are not under her headstone, and whether I should try.

"Welcome back," Paris greets me when I enter the library and find her at the main desk. Her chocolate locks are in a ponytail today. "Sage mentioned you might be visiting us."

The small-town library is cool and quiet, the same kittens I saw in December playing with a stuffed fish under the desk. They haven't grown, and I assume it's due to whatever magick the place is filled with.

"Good to see you." I look past her to the ghost floating behind her right shoulder. "You, too, Iula."

Paris' grandmother smiles. Her hands flutter in the air. "Did you get the ghost out of the minister?"

"Not yet." Luckily, there are only two patrons in the place and neither within earshot. "I have to find something besides drowning him to do it."

She adjusts her cat-eye glasses and grows solemn. "Tricky business that. You're wise to look for an alternative."

"Do you have any?" I ask hopefully.

Paris rises and comes around the desk. "Would you like us to research it?"

I join her as she leads me to a door inside her office. "Yes, please."

Once we're inside the secret elevator, she pulls the metal gate across and then an inner door. There are no buttons—it only goes up or down one floor. The compartment descends rapidly to the underground library that is a match for the one above it.

This version isn't filled with the latest bestsellers, however. Volumes of ancient texts and local histories line wooden shelves twice as tall as me, and seem to be never-ending, disappearing into the shadowy depths.

"How's Sherlock?" I ask as we exit and I glance at the tables and chairs scattered about. An assortment of ghosts reside here, but none pay us any heed, and there's no detective in sight.

Paris leans toward me and lowers her voice. "Grumpy as ever."

Iula hovers on my other side. "He seemed genuinely happy when he was assisting you and your guardian angel with solving mysteries. What happened?"

I'm at a loss, but assume Persephone did something to upset him. "Wish I knew. I miss him."

"Perhaps you can sweet talk him into helping you with this," Paris offers.

"Perhaps. I could really use his skills about a symbol I found that's linked to my family."

Paris perks up. "Such as a sigil?"

A woman nearly identical to her approaches us with a wave. "You must be Ava." She extends a hand. "I've heard so much about you."

London's hair is shorter and curlier, but her eyes and the tilt of her mouth are a match for her sister and grandmother. I shake her hand. "Thank you for meeting with me on short notice."

"Anytime." She turns toward a set of long tables and motions us over. "I've already laid out several volumes of witch histories that might prove insightful about your forebears and Redemption DeBane."

The three of us follow "Do any mention a curse?" I inquire.

"The DeBane family is well known for their hexes and curses.

They did a lot of black magick in Scotland and here once a few of them migrated."

Nice family.

"You don't cross the DeBanes," Iula states.

She says it in present tense. "I take it some are still around?"

London nods. "Afraid so, although most of those don't have the magick in their veins like the original families. It's diluted after centuries of disuse and them hiding from the world. The current DeBanes don't even know their own history anymore."

Sounds like a good thing to me. I scan the four texts she's laid out. Two are huge, the leather bindings cracked and flaking. The others appear more recent, although still quite old. "Where should I start?"

"Do you have a picture of the symbol?" Paris asks. "I can research that while you're reading about Redemption."

I haul out my phone and show her the photos I've amassed. "I think it has something to do with my grandmother's death and rebirth in cat form. Does that even make sense?"

Both sisters chuckle, as if that's a dumb question. It is, I suppose, to this pair, who deal with the invisible world of magick every day.

"Oh, that's a thistle bound with a Celtic triquetra." Paris thumbs through the photos again. "Was you grandmother from Scotland or Ireland?"

"Scotland. What's a triquetra?"

"A triangle knot," she explains. "It's not obvious with the thistle intersecting the threads. Very unusual design, and I suspect a custom one. She was most likely attempting to protect and bind at the same time."

Protect her family from Redemption, and bind her and Samuel together for eternity. Makes sense.

"There is a lot of great folklore on thistles and their magickal properties, as well as the triquetra." She returns my phone. "I'll grab some books for you."

Iula goes with her and London motions me to a chair. "Shall we start?"

I don't have much time, and these books aren't loanable. They have to stay in this library. *Sherlock*, I call mentally, taking a seat and glancing around, *I sure could use your help*.

Not even a heartbeat later, he says, "Hello, Ava."

He hovers at the end of the table, his odd spectacles and vintage woolen attire a welcome sight. "Where have you been?"

He appears to also sit, nodding at London, and glancing over the assortment of texts. "Here and there."

Persephone appears at that moment, glaring at him. "Now you show up?"

Has she been watching me? "You're one to talk," I say to her. "Where have *you* been?"

"Looking for him," she spouts, pointing. "We need help with another ghost."

He barely glances at her. "So I hear. From the sounds of it, you have more than one causing problems."

Her fists go to her hips, today clad in a bright blue skirt with beads in a wave pattern. "This is serious, Sherlock. Are you going to put aside our differences and help, or not?"

A long-suffering sigh issues from his mouth. London and I exchange a silent look, and drop our gazes to the books, as if we aren't witnessing this lovers' quarrel.

"It would be better if you let me handle this," he tells her, and I cringe.

Sure enough, she goes ballistic. "You? The most unreliable spirit I've ever met?"

"Shh." London glares from one to the other. "If you're going to fight, take it outside. This is a library, you know, and Ava has work to do."

Neither appears remorseful, but Persephone slinks into the chair opposite Sherlock. "I'll save you some time. After searching into the past that is available to me, I found that

Redemption and her immediate family left Salem during the witch trials. Snuck out in the middle of the night."

"I already know that," I tell her.

Her top lip quivers and she glares at me. "Patience, Ava."

"Sorry." I give her a nod to continue, even though I'm short on the stuff. "Please, do go on."

"No, you misunderstand. Patience was Redemption and Samuel's eldest daughter. They moved south, and Redemption kept tabs on Samuel and Tabitha. She cursed them and their offspring, as you know, but years later, when Patience learned they were thriving in Thornhollow, she felt it wasn't enough. She wanted her father and Tabitha to suffer."

A streak of protectiveness floods my system. "What did she do?"

"Your grandmother was just as strong in the Craft as the DeBanes and she thought she and Sam were safe for a long time, thanks to her own spells. She never realized Redemption's generational curse was in place, but through divination, she did learn about Patience's quest to cause harm to your family. She created a symbol of protection, and it also caused any harm cast by Patience to turn back upon her."

"The triquetra and thistle."

She nods.

Paris returns with a botanical volume and sets it open in front of me to a page with an illustration of several varieties of the plant. "Thistle represents bravery, devotion, durability, strength, and determination. People believed its powers would help you overcome the most stalwart enemy, and it could be used as a warning against unwanted meddling."

"Also the knots of the triquetra have no beginning and no end, representing eternity," Sherlock adds. "They can represent earth, air, and water, or—"

"Life, death, and rebirth," Iula finishes. "Your grandmother wanted to assert her power over the family throughout all time and space."

I sit back, my mind spinning. "But what's with Tabitha's bones being buried under the time capsule?"

Sherlock gives me an encouraging, if slightly exasperated, look. "Think, Ava. A time capsule. Eternity. It all goes hand in hand with her wishes. She's bound herself to the town and your kin, to be your guardian forever."

Wow. I can't wrap my mind around it.

"That's a nice theory," Persephone says, "but it's not true."

"How do you know?" Sherlock and I ask at the same time.

"Because the bones you discovered aren't Tabitha's."

I sit up straighter. "Then whose are they? They can't be Samuel's. The forensics expert says they're female."

"They are, indeed, a woman's." Her eyes glitter in the dim light as if she's willing me to connect the dots. "But not your grandmother's."

"Redemption?" I guess.

A shake of her head. "Close."

And then it dawns on me. "Patience?"

She winks. "See? If you pay attention to my clues, you can figure things out."

My stomach sinks, not because she's right, but I have another thought—one I don't like. "Did Tabitha...kill her?"

"Not per se. Patience did come to Thornhollow and tried to cause harm."

"The curse," Sherlock says. There's a hint of admiration in his voice. "Patience tried to harm Tabitha or one of the family, and it rebounded on her."

"Solid witchcraft." Iula nods with an impressed look.

Her granddaughters grin. Paris closes the botanical book. "*Good* witchcraft, I'd say."

❧

THAT EVENING, I'M DOWN AT THE HOMESTEAD, RUNNING MY fingers over the symbol on the fireplace. Tabby strolls in. "Nice work, grandma," I say to her. "Why was Patience wearing your ring when you buried her?"

She slides against the fireplace bricks, arching her back. No answer there.

"I'm guessing you put it on her after you discovered she was dead, determined to bind her to the spell to keep us all safe. That was the magick Samuel's upset about, that and using the cat's nine lives to keep you somewhat immortal, isn't it?"

She yawns and walks through a shaft of soft light coming through the high window. The sun is going down and Moxley is waiting to head up to the house for chow. Logan will be here any minute, and I've got dinner made. I was too tired and keyed up to cook, so sandwiches it is.

As the dust motes dance around her fur, my phone rings. It's Daddy. "Hey, thought you'd be at the mystery dinner by now," I say.

"I am. We've got a problem."

I go on high alert, my feet already heading for the house. "What is it?"

Moxley joins me, his body rocking with the effort to run and keep up. Daddy sounds quite upset. "Louise has been stabbed."

"What?" Chills run over my body.

"It was no accident. Someone nailed her right in the back."

"Is she...dead?"

He lets go of a tight sigh. "No, but she could have been if we hadn't found her in time."

"Oh, no. Do you know who did it?"

"There are a dozen people who are potential suspects. Landon and I are interviewing them now. Can you come get your mother and take her home for me?"

"Of course."

"Oh, and Ava? The weapon was the knife."

My footsteps falter. "THE knife? From the capsule?"

"Louise convinced Landon to put it on display tonight with the other items."

I find my footing again and pick up my pace. "I'm surprised he would do that."

"Any crime it was used for is hundreds of years old. He didn't see any issue with it."

"Plus, he's sweet on Louise," Persephone said. She's perched on the back porch.

Him, too? I wave her away so Mox and I can pass. "I'll be there in five."

$$\text{❧} \quad 18 \quad \text{❧}$$

The county forensics investigators are leaving when I arrive, Daddy escorting the two man-one woman team out.

"Did they find fingerprints on the weapon?" I query him as I rush up the steps.

He opens a massive door to the mansion, ushering me inside. "It's on its way to the ER with Louise, I'm afraid, still in her back. The doctor told Stout and Wes to leave it and he would remove it under controlled circumstances. They don't know what kind of damage it may have done, and keeping it where it was seemed safest."

My stomach rolls. Our minister moonlights as an EMT, along with Wesley Kauffman and a few others. "They left it *in?*" My voice echoes through the foyer and I flinch at the screech it makes.

"They did, and while I stressed to the crew that we needed the handle preserved for prints, that wasn't their main concern, and for good reason. We do have plenty on the display case where the knife was with the remaining items, but I'm sure those will only match Louise and those who work here."

"Was Reverend Stout acting normal?"

A nod. "That he was."

That brings a modicum of relief. A murmur drifts through the double doors off to the right. "Are the suspects in there?"

"Landon is doing interviews. He's placed those who were not in the formal dining hall when the attack occurred into the receiving parlor"—he points in the direction of the entrance—"while the others remain in the dining room. I'm acting as witness to the interrogations." His finger switches to indicate the hallway beyond the large curved staircase on the left. "Your mother is in the kitchen, making tea and helping Buster clean a few things. I'll catch up with you later."

It's been years since I've been inside the Historical Society, and normally I would take my time and gawk at the balcony above, and inspect spaces like the powder room discreetly hidden behind a pocket door. Tonight, I shiver at the ghosts I see from the corner of my eye, and have no desire to walk around alone.

Mama has no intention of leaving when I locate her in the main kitchen, close to the dining hall. "Someone has to be in charge," she tells me. "That would be me."

Of course it would.

"We didn't even get to enjoy dessert," Buster says, absent-mindedly. "I do hope she's okay."

"No one's heard about Louise's condition yet." Mama puts the kettle on and marches into the pantry. She reemerges with a box of tea bags. "Nash contacted her sister, who lives in Atlanta, but Louise doesn't have any relatives locally."

"How long will it take her sister to get to the hospital?" Buster asks.

"Probably an hour," I tell him.

"She's tough," Mama states, plopping the bags on a tray and beginning to load the dishwasher with glasses. "She'll pull through, don't you worry."

"I should have gone with her." He seems despondent and my heart hurts for him, unrequited love and all that. "What if she's scared?"

"She was conscious when the ambulance arrived?" I ask.

"Oh, yes," Buster says with a wan smile. He scrapes food from a plate into the garbage and hands the dish to Mama. "They warned us not to remove the knife, so we kept her propped up and she was going on and on about ruining the dinner. Nuttiest thing I ever saw, her sitting on the bench at the front window with a knife in her back."

Ouch, that must have hurt. I would have been freaked out. I touch his arm in a show of support. "Have you been interviewed already? If so, I'm sure Detective Jones would let you leave so you could see her."

Buster clamps his teeth together and grabs another dirty dish. "He told me to stick around. Wants to ask me more questions once he's done with the others."

The kettle whistles and Mama sets the plate into the dishwater, then pours the hot water into a carafe. "Buster was in the restroom when it happened."

His knuckles turn white on the dish. "No alibi," he adds with a sneer. "Can you imagine *me* stabbing Louise in the back?"

"Of course not." I take the plate from him and add it to those to be washed. "Surely, Jones doesn't think...?"

Mama gives a tiny shake of her head, loading antique tea cups on the serving tray with the carafe and a silver sugar and cream set. "He's covering his bases, that's all. Louise didn't get a look at the perpetrator, so the detective has to nail down exactly where everyone was at the time the incident happened."

"Where was Louise?"

Buster stares off into the distance. "The library. They set up the items from the capsule in there. She cleared a whole case Sunday and had it moved there because of the double entryways. She thought so many people would want to get a look at them, it would improve traffic flow."

"She told you all that?"

He avoids my eyes. "I helped her move the case."

Baylor bursts in, her coat open and flying out behind her. "I came as soon as I heard. Are you okay?"

Buster hugs her. "I'm fine. Thanks for coming. It's Louise we have to worry about."

Baylor acknowledges me and Mama. "How did this happen?"

"Buster can fill you in." Mama hands the tray to me. "Help me with this, would you, please, dear?"

I follow her out and she lowers her voice in the hallway. The floor creaks under our feet and the sconces give a soft, yellow glow to her face. "He's in love with her, you know. Louise."

"So I've heard, but Mama, he was arguing something fierce with her at the Beehive just yesterday. He was upset about her taking the items for the Society and not allowing Baylor to display them at the library. Why would he yell about it then and there, when he already knew about her plans on Sunday?"

Mama frowns. "Good question. Seems odd to make a public display of it, too. That's so not like him."

In the front room, we distribute the tea, several of the actors present and still in costume. "Got any of that whiskey to go with it?" one of the men asks.

It's the guy from the unveiling. Mama waves him off. "Don't be silly, Austin. We're not spiking our tea tonight, and especially not with a vintage bottle."

"Seems like as good of a time as any," his companion mumbles, and I recognize Candace, Mama's assistant. Her skirts swish as she sits beside him on a visitor's sofa. "When can we go, Dixie? You know we didn't have anything to do with what happened."

Mama gives her a warm smile. "As soon as Detective Jones has all the information he needs. He most certainly appreciates your patience, as do I."

"I didn't realize you were in the theater," I say to Candace.

Her heavy makeup is settling in the creases. Her cheeks are stained with bright rouge that looks garish under the light in here. "It's something to do in this town."

Austin squeezes her knee through her skirt. "You didn't even get to kill me."

She chuckles. "Maybe later."

"You were the murder victim?" I ask him.

He doesn't even glance at me, moving his hand an inch higher on her leg and staring into her grinning face. "Yep, and Candace was the killer."

They seem entirely too exhilarated by their roles. "Cool," I say, sounding like Rosie and Jenn.

Mama glances around at those who haven't taken tea. "Anyone else?"

"I'm hungry," one of the actors whines. "Is any of the food left?"

Mama picks up the tray. "I'll check."

I follow her to the parlor where the rest of the attendees are waiting at the large dining table. There's still plenty to eat, even though most of the participants no longer have plates in front of them. The exception is Amos Butterfield who is enjoying a heap of almost every dish available. "The asparagus in butter cream is divine," he states when we enter.

"Queenie is an amazing cook," Mama replies. "I'm so glad you're enjoying her cuisine."

Bis is there, as is Sage. I couldn't be more surprised. They acknowledge me and I smile at them. A woman moves to the side where Mama rests the tea tray. The two strike up a conversation as my phone rings.

I want to chat with Bis and Sage, but it's Logan. "Have to take this." I point to the phone. "I'll be back in a moment."

They nod, Sage looking bored as Bis leans on the fireplace and flicks glances at her. That boy has it bad, and I hope it won't be another case of unrequited love.

The Society mansion is a rambling old thing filled with solemn portraits, books that haven't been opened in decades, musty furniture, and assorted collections from times past. "Hey," I say to Logan, wandering down the hall and into a room on the west side, away from prying ears. The door is a pocket slider and exceptionally heavy. I have to stick the device between my shoulder and ear to open and then close it behind me. "Sorry I'm not home."

I relate the details about the dinner and attack. I also mention the weird matter with Buster. "I don't know how long I'll be here. If Mama refuses to leave, she might as well stay until Jones sends Daddy home, so I could be there sooner rather than later."

"Why would someone stab Louise?" He sounds as dumbfounded as I feel.

The interior smells like the older section of the library. A tall window lets in light from the street but I flip the switch on the wall. "Been asking myself the same thing. She wasn't entirely easy to get along with, but..."

Large glass lamps overhead spotlight walls of books. A display case with the time capsule items is front and center on a threadbare wool rug.

"Ava?"

"I'm here," I say, moving toward it. Jones will kill me if he finds me in here, but I keep my hands away from the glass even though the forensics team has dusted for fingerprints. Inside are the items with markers, explaining what they are. The knife is missing, of course, but so is another item. "The whiskey."

"What?" Logan asks.

"The liquor is missing," I tell him. "Look, I gotta go. I'll call you back."

"I'm coming over there. Stay with the others. Whoever stabbed Louise is still running around."

True. "See you in a few," I tell him and we disconnect. "Sherlock?" This is definitely his area of expertise. I bite my lower lip, nearly bouncing on the balls of my feet when he doesn't appear. "I need you. Please."

He pops in, startling me. No matter how many times I work

with spirits, they always manage to do that. "How may I be of service?"

"I've got what I believe is an attempted murder. The suspect is most likely still here in the house." I haul the heavy door open. "You in?"

He adjusts his spectacles and lifts his chin, seeming to think it over. "Quite," he answers, and floats through the doorway.

❦ 19 ❦

"Take this to those in the front room," Mama instructs when she catches me in the hall. She shoves a new tray laden with biscuits, cheese, and fruit into my arms.

Sherlock doesn't stop. "I need to talk to Daddy," I tell her, as he floats toward the front. I shove the tray back.

"After you deliver this." She gives me *the look*. The one that makes me twitch. "Those folks had their night ruined and didn't even get to finish a meal. They're all worried about Louise. It'll only take you a minute."

Butterfield appears. Bis and Sage are behind him. "There you are." He smiles at me, a piece of food caught in his mustache. "As long as we're stuck here for a while, I'd like to pick your brain."

"Maybe some other time." I'm all smiles as I put the tray between us and move around him. "We have food to deliver."

I tip my head at Bis and Sage, and they get the hint. Bis takes the tray and we hoof it away, Mama coming to my rescue by asking the author if he'd like dessert.

"I saw Sam," Bis says under his breath. "Lots of bananas in this place, but he was here, too."

At this news, I divert from our path and draw them into the kitchen. Luckily, Buster and Baylor are gone. "Where?" I ask.

Bis tips his chin over his shoulder. "In that room back there with the display."

"Louise walked all of us through the library before dinner officially started," Sage adds, glancing around the enormous kitchen. "I sure would like to get back in there and look at their collection of books."

"We stick together, okay?" I scan for Sherlock, don't see him. "Whoever attacked Louise is still running loose. Who knows what else they might try, especially if they think we're onto them."

Bis nods, glancing at Sage. She shrugs, and I notice she rubs the pendant hanging around her neck. "I'm not scared."

Probably not, since she's no doubt cast a protection charm on herself. I hope it extends to Bis as well. "Did anyone act odd at dinner?"

Sage makes a face. "Honestly? I mean, they're all a little odd."

Helpful. I lower my voice to just above a whisper. "Did you notice Austin, the actor, doing or saying anything strange?" Their blank faces tell me they don't know who I'm talking about. "Okay, look, he's in the parlor. I'll point him out when we go in there. Let me know if you remember him being secretive or saying anything unusual to Louise."

Assenting nods let me know we're on the same page again. We resume our trek and halt outside the parlor. I open the door.

Two steps in, I stop dead. The lights glare off the dark window throwing an odd shadow over a couple in front of it. I swear one of them is Louise.

Then Mama turns and catches me staring. "There you are," she says. "Where have you been?"

Butterfield is next to her and he pivots, too. Regaining my composure, I scan the rest of the faces, stomach falling. Austin is gone.

"Where did he go?" I pointedly look at the others.

"Who?" Mama asks.

"Austin." Candace is gone as well. "Where are he and Candace?"

The earlier hungry actor eyes the food and moves toward Bis and the tray. "They had an errand to run. They'll be back."

Sure they will. "I thought no one was supposed to leave."

No one else appears concerned. "Who was going to stop them?" another actor asks.

I turn and walk out, going in search of Daddy.

Cutting across the foyer, I run into Logan coming in. He hugs me and frowns down into my face. "What's the latest?"

There's not much to tell, other than my theory that Austin has absconded with the whiskey. His sidekick may have helped.

"That doesn't make him a suspect in Louise's attack," Logan argues.

I motion him to follow me. "I need to find Daddy."

He and Detective Jones are in what was once an informal living room. It's just the two of them when Logan and I arrive.

"Austin,"—I don't know his last name—"the actor who was to play the victim, left. I think he stole the whiskey that was in the time capsule. Did you already talk to him?"

"He what?" Jones stands from the chair he's sitting in. He's dressed in a suit and tie. The tie has been loosened and hangs crooked. "Did you see him take it?"

I shake my head. "He's the one who asked about it at the unveiling ceremony and he mentioned it again earlier when he was in the parlor. The bottle is gone."

Daddy and Jones take off for the library, Logan and I following. "No one was allowed in here," Jones bellows, glaring at me, once we're all inside the room. "It's a crime scene."

"I didn't know. I accidentally stumbled in when I took a call from him." I point at Logan. "That's when I saw it was missing. Now Austin and Candace have left."

Daddy frowns at Jones. "You spoke to Candace, didn't you?"

"Yeah, but not the kid."

"How'd he get in the case?" Daddy eyeballs it. "It was locked, right?"

Jones runs a hand down his face and shakes his head. "Louise never secures anything around here, except the front entrance."

"She shouldn't need to," I add.

"Not necessarily," Bis says from the door.

"What do you know?" Jones motions him in. Sage isn't with him now. "Tell me."

He takes a single step inside. "When Dad and I were working on the leak this morning, she was showing off the items to several folks, including Baylor and Buster. That mystery author came in and mentioned she really should be more careful with the items. They could fetch a lot of money with collectors. Baylor agreed, and then she and Louise got into an argument. Louise told Baylor she was paranoid, but when Buster said he thought it was a good idea to lock up the time capsule stuff, she backed off and said she'd think about it."

"So the thief could have snuck in here, planning to steal one of, or all of the collection," Daddy says. "Louise may have interrupted him and that's when he struck."

"Who would stab someone over a bottle of liquor?" Sage appears and ambles inside, her eyes running over the shelves of books. "Seems a little extreme."

"People have committed murder for less," Jones states. "And I swear the bottle was in there when I found Louise."

"*You* found her?" I ask.

He seems defensive. "She invited me in here during dinner to..." He clears his throat and I swear his cheeks flush. "She wanted to recruit me to join the Society."

Uh huh. I bet that's what they talked about. "Does Buster know?"

Jones rears back slightly. "Buster? Yeah. Everyone knows I found her."

"Did he know that you're sweet on her?"

Jones' eyes narrow. "We're friends, that's all."

Later, on the way home, I turn all of it over and over in my mind. "Is the whiskey thief the same person who stabbed Louise?" I ask out loud. "If so, why did he try to kill her? Is Jones right that she interrupted his robbery?"

Sherlock is in the passenger seat; Logan driving behind me. "Stabbing requires the perpetrator to get up close and personal," the ghostly detective states. "An act of passion. You know who that points to."

Buster. "No, it can't be him."

My sidekick doesn't question who I'm referring to. "You may not want to believe it is, but you need more to rule him out. What about his sister? She seems quite emotional."

Baylor wouldn't hurt a fly, would she? "I don't think she has it in her."

Jones and Daddy have gone to track down Austin. I'm betting they'll find an empty bottle, too. Or maybe he planned to sell it, like Bis said had been mentioned. Either way, he doesn't seem a likely candidate for the attack either.

Could it be Candace?

I can't find a motive for either of them, outside of perhaps Louise interrupting the theft. It's a possibility, but not a good one.

I stew more, arriving home to a dark house. It's nearly midnight and Logan walks me to the front porch. The gargoyles and knocker start babbling and I ignore them, opening the door to let Moxley out. He greets Logan and rushes down the steps, ready to go home.

"See you in the morning," Logan says with a kiss.

I watch him and Moxley cross the street, Sherlock entering the house.

"He's here," the knocker hisses.

"I know. I invited him." Logan unlocks his office then waves and I return it. "Be nice."

I start to go inside, exhausted but hoping Sherlock and I can hash this out.

"No, not him," one of the gargoyles says. "Him!"

When I glance back over my shoulder, my heart falters.

"Hello, Ava. I've been waiting for you." Reverend Stout is at the landing. I didn't even hear his footsteps. He clasps his hands in front of him, his face stony and his eyes lifeless. "We need to get the devil out of you."

20

"Get in," Persephone yells, appearing next to me. "Now!"

I trip over the threshold and feel Stout's hands brush my arms as he lunges for me. I go down on a knee, and swing wildly back at him when his fingers dig into my shoulder.

The knocker yells, along with the gargoyles, and my guardian angel seems to be trying to grip the man's coat. It's Tabby, though, who helps me, when she jumps and attaches herself to Stout's leg.

He releases me and I scramble away, holding the door to keep me upright. Stout screeches in pain and bends to grab Tabby by her scruff. I swing the heavy wooden door at his head.

The contact knocks him backwards. He staggers, one hand going to his head, the other attempting to pry Tabby and her claws from his leg.

More than once, my great-grandmother has defended me. I understand her quest to keep her descendants safe on a much deeper level now, and boy, do I appreciate it wholeheartedly at the moment.

"The cross!" Persephone yells at me. "Get it!"

Stout lands on his side, unable to dislodge the feline, and blinking from the blow to the head. His feet are still in the doorway and I can't close it. The bag with the cross and black kyanite is on my desk and I fly across the foyer. Grabbing the whole thing, I rush to the scene.

He pitches onto his back and stares up at the overhang. His hands work, clenching and unclenching, as he shakes his head as if to clear it. His eyes no longer have that flat look to them, but maybe that's because I've concussed the poor guy.

"My," Sherlock says behind me "your life is full of interesting people."

Ripping open the bag, I grab the cross and the crystals tumble around my feet. I hold it out at Stout. "You're not in your right mind, Reverend. It's the ghost hitchhiker. Get away from me."

A misty substance begins to seep from him into the air. The face of the possessing ghost forms, straining to stay attached. It's as if Marvin's being pulled out of the minister by invisible hands.

I bend and press the cross against Stout's chest. "Get out of him, Marvin. This isn't right. You need to get over your petty self and move on to the afterlife!"

Behind me, the crystals vibrate and several begin to rise. They encircle me and Reverend Stout. I peek at Persephone but she shakes her head at my questioning look. She's not doing it.

Tabby retracts her claws and slinks away. Nothing in her cat body suggests she's doing it either.

Marvin gives a howl. The mist stretches to the max. I continue pressing against Stout. "Get out, get out, get out," I chant. "Go to the light, go to the light, go to the light."

There's a *pop* and Marvin is gone.

I sink back, limp with relief. The crystals fall from the air, landing on the wood slats.

Stout rises to his elbows. His eyes are normal and full of questions. "What happened?"

I stagger to my feet. "We had to get that ghost out of you, Reverend."

Something flickers across his face. "I feel like I'm not myself these days."

"I bet you do." Reaching down, I offer a hand to help him stand. "Why don't you come inside?"

He refuses it, coming to his hands and knees. "I need to go."

"Reverend..."

Equilibrium still off, he half falls down the stairs. I start to go after him, but Persephone jets in front of me. "Let him be."

"Is Marvin gone for good?"

"He didn't cross over," she states firmly. "He'll be back."

"All the more reason I have to go after Stout."

"You can't help him tonight." She nods toward the porch on my left. "Deal with him first."

I glance at the rocking chairs. My grandfather is watching the exchange from the shadows in the corner. He nods in acknowledgement. "That was a fine display. Are you well?"

I laugh, a dry, humorless sound. Glancing at the now unmoving crystals, I ask Persephone, "What kind of magick was that?"

Her gaze flicks to Samuel. "His."

My brows hit my hairline and I swing around to face him. "You're a practitioner of the Craft, too?"

"The young man earlier tonight claimed you needed to speak to me."

"Nice deflection." My eyes feel gritty, my knee stings. I gather the crystals. "I need to know what happened to Patience," I tell him. "Let's go inside."

Surprisingly, he follows me in, using the door like Sherlock did. The two ghosts size each other up in the main room and Tabby hurries to the kitchen. Arthur and Lancelot are curled up in the display window, seemingly unconcerned about what just happened.

Persephone floats along with me as I head to the desk. "It was his magick, I'm sure of it. I didn't realize he was a mage."

The white bag is in pieces. I pick them up and crumple them

in my hands. "I don't even know what that is, and at the moment, I don't care."

"A man of great learning," Sherlock calls to me. "A wizard or magician."

I lock the door and toss the paper into the trash. Then I take a seat in the living room. "Tabby?" I call.

Samuel examines the fireplace and Sherlock and Persephone sit on the matching chairs, eyeballing each other. Every time one catches the other looking, they glance away. "Stop it," I say. I've run out of patience. "You two are good together and there's no reason to let trivial things get in the way. Quit making yourselves miserable and forgive whatever's torn you apart."

Tabby slinks in, her gaze on Samuel. He acts as though he isn't eavesdropping on my lecture and is fascinated with the pictures on the mantle. When she gets close, however, even I can feel the electricity between them. His gaze immediately snaps to her. "You were marvelous, love."

She purrs and strokes his leg with her body. Bending, he scoops her up and they stare into each other's eyes. It's rare that a ghost can move solid objects like that, and I wonder if that's part of his mage-ness or Tabitha's magick.

My great-grandfather is a wizard, his wife, a witch. Who needs Harry Potter?

When Samuel gives her a sexy smile, I realize they're using telepathy. Her purrs echo around the room, the zing and sizzle between them ratcheting up another ten degrees.

O-kay. I clear my throat. "You were *both* marvelous, and you can catch up later. At the homestead, please, not in my house, thank you." They ignore me, still lost in their soulmate connection. "Can we talk about Patience now?"

Resigned, he puts her down. "My daughter, you mean?"

"Tell me what happened with her. She's the one buried under the time capsule, correct?"

Samuel sneaks a peek at Tabby, who hops onto the footrest. Again, it's as though they're using ESP.

"This would be easier if you would..." He rolls his hand at her. "Change."

Ho, boy. I grab the afghan from the back of the couch just in time. The marmalade cat goes from ten pounds of fur and whiskers to a full-grown woman, taller than me, and much more filled out.

Handing her the covering, I give her one of Mama's looks. "Thank you for helping me with Reverend Stout, but for the love of all that's holy, can you not do that in front of company?"

She glances at Sherlock and Persephone, who are now scanning the walls and ceiling, avoiding staring at the naked woman in front of them. "Are ye prudes, then?"

Her accent is lovely and I like hearing it, but it's rude to put us on the defensive. "There's a thing called modesty, grandmother."

"You are an extraordinary creature," Samuel says, ogling her.

She winks at him and gives me a gloating smile, reluctantly tucking the afghan around her. "Patience tried to kill him," she states matter-of-factly.

I resume my seat. "With magick?"

"And poison. She was determined."

"Did your spell rebound on her and cause her death?"

"Ye can put money on it." She looks proud and reaches for Samuel's hand. "What daughter of worth attempts patricide?"

My grandfather's face softens. "She was ruined by her mother. I welcomed her to our home, believing she meant well. It all went so wrong."

"You took Patience in?" I'm shocked. "I thought you tried to get your kids from Redemption but it didn't work."

"I did," he assures me, "and you are correct. She came to us as an adult. Showed up on our doorstep, tried to harm me, and ended up causing it to herself."

Persephone and Sherlock are listening as raptly as I am.

"She nearly succeeded in her task," Tabitha states, continuing. "She sent her familiar, with poison on her claws, to scratch him. The cat was repelled by my spell, however, and attacked her instead."

Samuel shifts and sits next to her on the footrest. "When Tabitha found Patience, she was five miles from town, trying to get back to her mother. The familiar had attacked her and she was dying a slow death. She'd fended off the beast and it was dying, too."

"She begged me to save it." Tabitha looks almost wistful.

Sherlock clears his throat. "She was dying and begged you to save her pet?"

Tabitha draws back, slightly haughty. "It was her familiar and she loved the creature. The innocent thing had only done her bidding; it wasn't evil itself."

"Tabitha saved it the only way she could," Samuel tells us.

With magick. "So those weren't the cat's bones that were found with Patience's skeleton?"

"O 'tis." Tabitha waves a dismissive hand. "That body couldn't be saved. I had to take the animal's essence, its spirit, and find another receptacle for it."

I frown. "Yours, I presume?"

"The spell was one I had no knowledge of prior to using, and I was unaware of its...drawbacks."

"It backfired on you?" I try to hide my amusement. "You ended up in a cat's body by accident?"

"So cool," Persephone says with more than a little adoration.

Tabitha's posture grows stiffer. "I intended to use its nine lives to extend my own. I was unprepared for the shifting abilities."

"You finished the cat off." I'm sure it had to be done, but *eww*. "With the knife?"

My grandmother lifts her chin. "When I removed the essence, it naturally died, and that cat served my purposes. Redemption's evil would never stop. The responsibility to save our family rested with me, and I was charged to fight it. The only reason ye be here, Ava, is because of my sacrifice."

"She has been the family protector all these years," Samuel agrees. "If not for her, you and yours would never have existed."

I don't doubt it. "Why bury Patience under the beech?"

"It was but a sapling." Now Samuel looks wistful. "The building you call City Hall was the general store and it faced east, not south. We buried her there so Redemption wouldn't find her, should she come looking."

"Aye, we suspected she would," Tabitha states with a nod.

Samuel nods too. "There was a crossroads there at the time, so perfect for our means."

"A good place to hold magick." Persephone seems impressed. "Why put the ring on her?"

Tabitha glances at Samuel's ghostly hands, his own band missing. "To bind her spirit and keep it front haunting us."

Not sure I understand that, but okay. Must have something to do with the sigil. "And the time capsule? Why bury it on top of her?"

"The general store was our town center then," Samuel tells me. "It was a coincidence that our leaders decided that spot, under that young tree, would be the perfect place to put it."

"I bet you had a few uncomfortable moments," Sherlock quips, "when they were digging up the ground."

My grandparents share a smile. "You are correct, my fellow." Samuel glances at all of us in turn. "The knife was my doing. My blood is on that cloth."

Tabitha touches his knee, which seems to solidify under her hand. "Ye never were truly gifted with the Craft, my love."

He makes a face. "My objective was to stay with you. I hated the thought of you alone. Your soul encased in a cat..." He gives a shudder.

"He performed a ritual to tie himself to the town," she explains, "so that after his passing, his spirit would stay, rather than moving on."

"Except he literally tied it to the time capsule," I theorize.

Samuel's face is slightly abashed. "I learned much from your grandmother about using protection magick and thought I could do more. I made an error in judgment."

"Magick is nothing to toy with," Tabitha chastises. "We've learned that, haven't we?"

My mind goes to Stout and the fact Marvin isn't gone forever. "Which brings up the fact that our current town minister has been, and may be again, possessed by a vengeful spirit. This is out of my league, and my comfort zone. I need help."

"What can we do?" Samuel asks without hesitation.

I tap my chin with a finger, an idea forming. I don't know much about magick, but I do know a little about ghosts. With this group of spirits backing me up, I may have a good chance to fix the issue and move Marvin along, while not causing any harm to Stout. "This may need some tweaking," I tell them, "but here's what I'm considering as Plan A."

I lay out my strategy and watch each of them ponder it.

"That might work," Tabitha says.

Persephone stands and winks at me. "Of course, it will. Trust me, your granddaughter, however many times removed, is one smart cookie. A little dense on occasion, but brilliant at others."

"Why, thank you, Persephone." Coming from her, that's quite a compliment, regardless of the insult it included. I glance around the room, meeting each person's eyes. "We'll reconvene tomorrow night after I talk to Daddy, okay?"

Nods and affirmations resound.

We've got ourselves a plan.

21

The next morning when I call Daddy, he's still looking for Austin. "We haven't located Candace, either," he tells me, "and your mother is a mess."

"You think something happened to them?"

"Sure. They got loaded and are sleeping it off somewhere."

Mama may have good reason to be upset. "Should we be worried?"

He sighs. "I've called the local hotels and checked the hospital. No one has seen or heard from them, but with what I understand from their family and friends, this isn't abnormal. Even Dixie has had issues with Candace not showing for work."

My fax beeps and I see the light blink. "She never said anything."

"To me, either. She likes the girl, didn't want to fire her."

I'm a bit surprised, considering how Mama is so demanding of most of us. The machine begins to print out a page. "How's Louise?"

"Coming home today. The blade didn't sink too far in and she's feeling good. Makes me think her attacker wasn't strong enough to drive it deep, or had a last minute change of heart."

I drink my coffee, my brain nibbling at that. "But you believe it was premeditated?"

"Seems that way. Landon is still entertaining the idea it could have been an act of convenience. The attacker was mad, grabbed the weapon on a spur of the moment whim, and struck."

"Do you like Austin for it?"

"Neither of us can see him doing it."

The fax is from Marla. She's handwritten several notes on it. "What if the attacker thought Louise was someone else?"

"Like who?"

I rub my temple, this week's lack of sleep making me sluggish. A headache is building behind my eyes. "I know this sounds daft, but the other night, when I saw Mama in a certain light, I thought she was Louise."

Daddy chuckles. "Don't tell her that."

"I'm serious. What if the attacker was waiting for Mama, heaven forbid, and didn't realize it was Louise until he or she had already stabbed her. You said they may have had a change of heart, right?"

"Hmm. That does shed a different light on things."

"Mama is well liked, but she does have an enemy or two in town. No telling who she's vexed and over what." Marla's note says to check my email, so I sit at the desk and pull it up. "Maybe you should have Jones put a security detail on her until we get this figured out."

"She'll love that," Daddy says under his breath. "But you're right, better safe than sorry. I'll play bodyguard, and she'll never have to know if she's not the target. If she is, I'll protect her."

I feel better. "Thank you."

He tells me he loves me and not to worry before we disconnect. I carry the mug and papers across the backyard to the B&B.

"A strong possibility for the Toad." I hand Rhys the listing. "It just went up and Marla says it won't last long."

The kitchen smells like warm blueberries and cream. Mitts

on, he pulls muffins from the oven and sets the pan on a cooling rack. "The pressure to figure this out is killing me." He tugs off the mitts and grabs the sheet. His eyes bounce up to mine. "Betty's going out of business?"

"She's moving to the mini-mall property." I share the details Marla had in her email. "Jo's Rental is, too, and Marla claims he's taking two slots to expand his offerings to include tourist items, like bikes and hiking gear. With the trails a block away, it could be a boon for his business."

"Betty's Floral Shop has been downtown forever. She really wants to relocate to the highway?"

"She's opening a garden center, so the extra outside space is perfect for it."

He brightens. "Okay then, seems we may have a winner. It's smaller than the metalworks building, but it'll be closer to the coffee bar and here. Could save me a lot of time not having to drive out and back every day."

"That's the spirit." I eye the muffins, stomach growling. "Plus, that old house has great atmosphere, much better than the metalworks, and it already has a kitchen. You can have the bar and seating downstairs and put your card readers upstairs. There are four bedrooms and a bath."

The corner of his mouth twitches and he gets that look in his eyes. It tells me he's dreaming about the potentials. He goes to the counter and lays down the listing. A stack of white dessert plates rests nearby and he places one of the cooling treats on it for me. "How soon will she be out?"

I break it in half, steam rising. "She's moving next week, and Marla believes she'd be agreeable to letting you rent it for now with the option to buy down the road."

He snags coffee for me, as well. "This could work out great. I'm excited."

Victory! At least on one front.

"Did your father arrest that Austin fellow?"

"Haven't located him yet. Candace either. Anyway, neither he nor Jones believe they had anything to do with the stabbing."

"Who *does* your dad suspect?"

"He didn't say, probably because he knows it will upset me."

Rhys makes a face. "It's Buster, isn't it?"

I let the coffee steam coat my face. "I'm worried it's Baylor."

"What?" He whacks me with a mitt. "She would never."

Amos Butterfield rushes in, suitcase in hand. "I'd like to pay my bill and I need a receipt."

Rhys hands me the cup. "You're going so soon?"

"My publisher needs me back in Dallas."

"But you're not supposed to leave town," I say around a bite. "Not until Louise's attacker is found."

He draws himself up a notch and stares down his nose at me. "Don't be ridiculous. I had nothing to do with that. You small-town people think everyone from the city is a scheming rat. I hardly have murder in my heart."

Rhys and I share a glance. What is he talking about? "I assure you, Mr. Butterfield, we hicks do not see you swanky big city folks that way," Rhys tells him with a giant smile and a wink, "but as Ava mentioned, you've been asked by our police department to stay until the mystery is solved."

Covertly, I take my cell from my pocket and text Daddy: *SOS B&B.* "What about the book signing at the library?" I ask, hoping to stall him.

"My schedule has changed and I must cancel."

I wonder if he bothered to notify Baylor. She'll be so disappointed. This sudden departure makes me unquestionably suspicious. "I'm really sorry to hear that," I say. "I was hoping to pick your brain about murder mysteries."

"I wish to pay my bill," Butterfield states again emphatically, ignoring my turning things around on him. "Are you going to tally it up or not?"

"Go ahead," I tell my friend. I shift so my back is to Butterfield and mouth *stall him.* Rhys nods.

Setting the cup in the sink, I turn to face the author. "Can I get you a muffin for the road? On the house, of course."

He sniffs, and I see the hankering for one in his expression. The man is definitely motivated by food. "I may be compelled to accept."

"I'll bring it right out."

Rhys leads him from the kitchen to the desk near the front door to take the man's credit card and provide the receipt he's no doubt turning into his publisher. Daddy responds to tell me he's on his way. I bag up a muffin and plan my next move.

Out in the drive, I linger with it near Butterfield's rental. He hustles from the B&B, fumbling with the keys. The fob beeps and the trunk pops open. He tosses the suitcase inside and slams it shut.

I hold up the bag, but jerk it out of his reach when he tries to take it. "I wonder if I could just ask you a question about your books."

He huffs and looks like he might murder me. "What?"

I resist the urge to step back. "*Murder In His Heart*. That's the title of your latest release, right?"

A curt nod. "The next one is *Murder In Her Heart*. That's the one I'm working on now. It's a fictional series based on true crimes. Why?"

"When you used that phrase earlier, what did you mean?"

His mustache quivers. "All humans have the capacity to kill, but it takes a trigger, and a strong one at that, for most to follow through."

"What kind of trigger?"

Annoyed, he glances around, as if the answer is in the landscape. "An emotion like jealousy, hate, anger. The biggies."

Thinking about the possible suspects, I can check a couple of those. "What about if someone isn't necessarily emotional, but gets caught doing something wrong, like stealing? They react simply to protect themselves."

"Well, of course, that's feasible, and I know what you're hinting at. The bottle of whiskey that went missing. You think the thief may have been caught in the act and planted that knife in your friend's back to escape. But Louise didn't see the person, right? He or she was hidden. Why not simply stay that way? Why attack her?" He shakes his head. "The killer had the knife already, and jumped her when she entered the room. That's premeditated, and that smacks of an emotional trigger. From what I've witnessed, she has several enemies and admirers. Your detective is one of them." Pride at his suggestion shows on his face.

I stare, dumbfounded, for a heartbeat. "You think Detective Jones did it? Please. He's an uptight rule follower. I'm not sure he even has emotions."

"How easy would it be for him to set up the other fellow, the city administrator, to take the fall? To make sure Louise wasn't fatally injured and to rescue the damsel in distress?"

He paints an ugly picture. "He would never do that."

"Now who's letting emotions cloud their perception?"

Come on, Daddy. Where are you? "So if you were to choose a killer, hypothetically, let's say for one of your books, it wouldn't be the mystery writer who comes to town and likes to do in-depth research on his characters?"

Oops, went too far. He narrows his eyes and shakes a finger in my face. "Rude *and* inappropriate. I tried to be nice to you, but I see how it is. You're making fun of me and accusing me of committing a crime."

If the shoe fits. "It was a joke. I didn't mean to offend."

He slides into the driver's seat. "Good day, Miss Fantome."

Daddy's still nowhere in sight, and I'm not letting him get away. Rhys has come on the porch and wrings his hands. *What now?* he mouths.

As the engine ignites, I race to the other side. Luckily, the door isn't locked. I fling it open and drop into the passenger seat. "I really am sorry."

Butterfield's neck goes red as beets and the color seeps up into his cheeks. "Get out!"

When I was a kid, Daddy told me that if someone was trying to kidnap me, never let them get me in a vehicle. If they did, he might never be able to find me. He told me to kick and scream and do whatever it took to get away or get help. I wonder now if Butterfield will drive off with me as his hostage. I'm not eight anymore, though, and I'm not scared of him. "But I'm not finished. You want to know what it's like to be a medium?"

I'm about to charge on when Persephone appears in the back. "Oh, Lord. Here we go."

I whip around and glare at her. "Shut up."

Some of the author's anger fades. He glances at the spot I spoke to. "Is there..." He gulps. "Is there a ghost in the car?"

"She's technically a guardian angel, but her help is questionable."

"Not fair," she chides. "You're a difficult charge."

"There *is* a ghost over at my place." I point to The Wedding Chapel. "He's my ancestor and he's a pill. Founded the town. If you want, I can set up an interview for you. He can tell you what it's like to be trapped in the time capsule for three hundred years."

Butterfield's eyes grow saucer size. "He was there, wasn't he? That's why you were acting so odd."

Persephone snorts. "Nah, she comes by that naturally."

"It's super fun being able to see and hear ghosts," I lie, nodding my head much too enthusiastically. "Just loads. They bop in and out at all hours, usually won't answer questions, and a few have tried to kill me and my family, or at least scare the you-know-what out of us."

"Do you help them cross to the other side?" he asks, warming to the interview. "*Is* there an afterlife? What is it like?"

"Cavalry is here," Persephone says and disappears.

I wonder if she planned on staying if the man took off with me. From the corner of my eye, I see a squad car racing toward us. A sigh of relief blows out my lips as Jones blocks Butterfield's escape.

The author goes ballistic once more, yelling as I bail and Rhys comes running to my side.

Daddy is riding with Jones and the two of them descend on Butterfield. He didn't actually leave town, but they read him the riot act and threaten to put him in jail.

He seals his fate when he shoves Daddy and grabs me. He gets ahold of my shoulders and shakes me hard, calling me names. "You tricked me!"

Talk about a trigger. My teeth clatter from the rough treatment, but a combination of my knee coming up to nail him between his legs, Rhys kicking him in the shin, and both Daddy and Jones grabbing his arms, stops any further assault.

When they yank him away, I stumble backward and nearly lose my balance. Rhys catches me and helps me to The Wedding Chapel, where we watch from the porch as Jones arrests Butterfield and forces him into the back of the squad car.

"Are you alright?" Daddy asks, rushing over a minute later.

"Fine," I say. "I'm pressing charges."

"You bet your green eyes you are."

We watch in solidarity as Jones drives off, Butterfield looking over his shoulder at me, his mouth working.

Rhys, an arm around my waist, gives me a squeeze. "You're amazing. I can't believe how brave you are."

The door knocker snorts. "Stupid is more like it."

The gargoyles laugh in agreement.

❦ 2 2 ❦

The next day, the book signing is off and Baylor is bummed.
Butterfield is cooling his heels in our tiny jail, the local
attorney—*ahem*, my fiancé—refusing to take his case, and his
own lawyer several states away. Word is, he'll be here later today.

Louise's prints were all over the knife, and the others lifted
from the handle are from an unknown source. Jones has
concluded it came from the original owner after checking it
against Butterfield's. The two didn't match, and a search hasn't
turned up anyone else's in the system.

I'd like to tell the detective he's correct about it belonging to
the owner—Samuel— but I decide to let it be. He'll never
believe me anyway.

The blood on the cloth is also from an 'unknown source,'
Daddy tells me, but definitely human, according to the forensics
report. Detective Jones seems relieved about the cold case being
a nonissue in light of the more current one; Daddy, disappointed.
I plan to tell him the details of what I learned from Sam and
Tabitha, but there hasn't been time, and they're still no closer to
figuring out who attacked Louise.

Austin and Candace finally turn up that evening. "Seems they
ran off to Mississippi and got married," Mama tells me over

dinner at Queenie's. "Detective Jones is questioning them now. Why don't you join them, Nash?"

Daddy adds ketchup to his plate and dips a fry in it. "Landon can handle it."

Logan joins us, kissing me as he slides into the booth. "What'd I miss?"

It's good to feel him next to me as we eat and talk. "Are you excited about tomorrow?" I ask Mama.

She swallows a mouthful of food. "With everything going on, I've barely thought about it, but yes, I am."

Daddy brushes his hand against her wrist. "Me, too."

"I used to watch that VHS tape of your wedding over and over," I reminisce. "I think that's what inspired me to start sketching dresses. What did you do with your wedding gown?"

"That ol' thing." She makes a face. "My mother picked it out and it just wasn't me. Willa didn't have any money when she married Saddler the following year, and she loved that style, so I gave it to her. It's probably still in her attic."

I put my fork down, an idea striking. "What didn't you like about it?"

"It's all lace and frou-frou. Very traditional Southern bride, with a high neck and too many layers of tulle. I prefer simple, elegant." She nods. "You know."

Baylor, Buster, and Louise come in to have dinner. They stop at our table and make small talk. It appears Louise is feeling fine, and the two women have made peace with each other for the moment. Buster can't stop smiling.

"I don't know what to do with all those books," Baylor tells us. "Butterfield's publisher sent a giant box of them last week, and now the guy's in jail. I spent money we didn't have setting this whole thing up and advertising it, and now that's down the drain. They better not ask me to mail them back!"

"He'll probably be even more famous after this," Buster comments. "The notorious mystery writer unjustly accused of attempted murder. I can see the headlines now."

"He was arrested because he attacked Ava," Daddy clarifies.

"And you," I add.

"I don't think that will play as well." Buster winks. "I'm just glad Louise is okay and things have worked out."

"The culprit is still loose," Logan reminds us.

Louise shakes her head. "I'm not worried. Detective Jones and Nash, here, will find the culprit, if they haven't already."

"You think it's Butterfield?" I'm surprised.

She shrugs. "He's a peculiar fellow, isn't he? I heard him and Candace talking about the murder mystery and he was insisting they had the motive all wrong. That her character, the killer, needed a stronger motivation. I mean, it's just a fun little game. He was quite livid about the 'lazy writing,' he called it, of their script."

Daddy perks up. "What did Candace say?"

"Not much. She got away from him." Louise says this as if she would have done the same. "She was polite and all, asked him a few questions and acted as if she was making notes on his ideas, but gave me the crazy signal"—she twirls a finger at her temple—"when she finally begged off and saw me watching."

"He's big on triggers." I wonder if Candace likes being married. "And getting under the skin of his characters."

"He does write a good mystery," Baylor says a bit dolefully. "I was hoping he'd sign a few extra copies and donate them so I could sell them at our next library fundraiser."

They leave us and take a table across the room.

"Ava and I were talking about having Reverend Stout join the ceremony," Daddy says casually to Mama. "Would be nice to have him give a blessing, and say a prayer. He was our original minister, after all. Might be polite to have him participate this time, too."

Her gaze flicks between us. "You two planning things behind my back?"

I drop my attention to the last of my meal and move it around with my fork. "We would never."

"Uh huh."

Daddy chuckles. "I believe our vicar is feeling a bit adrift these days, and us leaving him out of this big event has caused a few hurt feelings."

Mama turns serious and lowers her voice. "He called our daughter an abomination in front of the whole town, Nash."

"He's not been feeling well," I interject, coming to the man's defense. "He'll be better tomorrow."

Daddy gives me a questioning look. I ignore it, and Logan mentions his current quandary. "About tomorrow. My family has had a slight change of plans."

I cringe. He must not have worked anything out with Helen.

"Oh?" Mama raises an eyebrow. "What's going on?"

Logan sets his napkin on the table. "Bad timing, I'm afraid."

"Out with it, Logan," Mama commands, seeing his reluctance to tell her. "Whatever it is, we'll work it out. Is your mother okay?"

He sits back and puts an arm on the top of the seat, his hand resting against my shoulder. "Chuck's coming home and has an announcement to make. Mother has decided to have a big family dinner for him."

Mama's eyes shutter slightly, even though she smiles. "Well, that's certainly understandable. You will be able to make the ceremony at four, though, right?"

"I'll be there. The rest of them...probably not. I'm sorry, Miss Dixie."

She dismisses his apology with another smile. "You're part of our family now, too, but yours must come first with something like this. Any idea what this news might be?"

"No clue," Logan admits. "I called him today and tried to weed it out of him, but he's keeping his cards close to his chest."

Queenie checks on us. "Did y'all save room for dessert?"

We're stuffed so she sends us home with slices of pie. Outside, I tell Logan I'll meet him at my place to pick up Moxley, and then I pull Daddy aside. "I have a plan to help

Reverend Stout, but I'm going to need the use of a jail for a short amount of time tonight."

"That's an odd thing to request." He gives me a wary grin. "Do I want to know?"

"I'll meet you at nine and give you the details then, okay?"

He glances at Mama in the front seat of his car. "What about watching her?"

"Bring her along. I have a job for her as well."

His face shows resignation. "What do I tell Landon?"

"He's not working tonight, is he?"

"He's on call."

"I'd prefer he stay away. I'll think of something."

Daddy looks troubled. "What about Butterfield? He's occupying one of those cells."

"Oh, he'll love the demonstration, trust me. He wants to know what it's like to be a medium? He's about to get a front row seat to the Ava Fantome show."

❦ 23 ❦

The stage is set with both humans and spirits when the minister arrives at the jail.

"So glad you could make it," Mama says out in the lobby. She's hip on my plan, and although I've left out a few details, she understands the seriousness of the situation.

"A funny place for us to meet," I hear Reverend Stout respond.

The iron bars of the cell I stand in are slightly rusted after years of humidity, along with wear and tear. Various visitors have left their marks on the walls and seat. Butterfield is signing copies of the books his publisher sent and watching us warily. When he asked what we were doing, I told him the truth—meeting Reverend Stout here to discuss tomorrow night's ceremony.

Tabby, in cat form, lounges on the bench, sharpening her claws on the wood. I can't see Samuel, Persephone, or Sherlock yet, but I know they're close and ready to assist once we have Stout and his ghost contained.

"Like I mentioned," Daddy chimes in, "I have to watch the prisoner overnight. We know it's unusual, but appreciate you coming here to chat with us about this."

The three of them appear and Stout stops, his bushy brows rising when he sees me and Logan in the largest cubicle. The door is open and we attempt to appear casual, like we sit around in jail cells often, gabbing about the weather and whatnot. Stout's face pales. "Ava? Logan?"

Logan nods. "Reverend. How are you?"

I give a wave and stand, holding out my hand as if to shake his, while staying in place. "Glad you could make it. Welcome to our makeshift planning room. I know it's a bit last minute, with the event tomorrow, but I wanted to get all of us together and nail down our itinerary."

Clutching his Bible close to this chest, he ignores my hand and sends his gaze around the space. "Isn't there an office we could use?"

Daddy closes in, motioning him to enter. "You couldn't fit two goats in these offices. Even as chief, I had to hold meetings in here, just to get all my staff in one room."

Mama sashays in without hesitation and wiggles her fingers, beckoning him to follow. "I'm so sorry about the misunderstanding regarding the renewal. Ava"—she points at me—"told us how upset you are, and we want to make it right."

Butterfield, behind me in the other cell, closes the cover of a book from the box. I mentioned I'd be willing to drop my charges if he signed them for Baylor to auction at her fundraiser, and he reluctantly agreed. Now he watches with great interest, sensing something is up, and I figure he'll be making notes before this affair is over. "I'm pretty sure this violates my rights," he says.

I spear him with a glare. "Keep going or my offer is void."

He curls a lip but returns to his business, turning his back on us.

Tabby hops down and makes her way to Stout's legs. He takes a step back when he sees her, no doubt remembering her sinking her claws into him last night, and shakes his head. "Something's not right. I think I should go."

I was afraid of this. "Daddy."

On my cue, my father grabs Stout and forces him forward.

"What is going on here?" Stout shouts.

Logan grabs the man's wrists. It's a tug-of-war for a heartbeat as the three wrestle, but Tabby pokes the minister in his calf, and he nearly jumps inside.

I grab the edge of his jacket as Daddy slams the door and locks it. The Bible falls and Stout yells, thrashing about. He shoves me away, but can't fend off Logan.

"Persephone!" I call.

Butterfield, realizing this is no meeting, jumps up and plasters himself against the far wall of his compartment. "You people are unhinged. What are you doing to that poor man?"

"Shut up," Mama says. "This is none of your business."

My guardian angel pops in, Samuel with her. "Get his arms through the bars," I instruct.

Logan wheels Stout around. I see the minister's eyes have turned glassy and I know Marvin is about to surface. The ghost isn't happy one bit about this trap, and I know he'll attack Logan, or anyone else, if he can.

Reverend Stout is no small man, and with Marvin's spirit controlling him, he knocks his shoulder into Logan, breaking his hold. I come at him from behind and throw all my weight into his backside. The force of the collision surprises him and he stumbles. His chest hits the metal bars and Logan and I each grab an arm, forcing his hands between them to the outside.

Daddy, ready and waiting, slaps a pair of handcuffs around his wrists.

Body on the inside and hands on the out, Stout—or I should say, Marvin—roars with anger. The sound of it sends an icy slice of fear down my spine.

"Get the salt," Persephone instructs.

Panting, I rush to the bag under the bench. I've brought the cross, crystals, salt, and holy water. As I follow her directions and form a circle with the salt around the minister inside the cell, Logan and Mama step away, watching.

Stout wails, Marvin flipping like he's a fish out of water. I stay clear of his legs so he doesn't kick me as I pour a thick line to surround him, and then hand the bag to Daddy, so he can finish it outside the bars.

"Did we miss anything?" a man's voice calls from the foyer. Bis and Sage appear, him looking excited, her not so much.

"Just getting started," I tell him.

Sage withdraws a book from her bag. "I found a spell that should work."

"*Should?*" Mama and I reply at the same time.

Opening to a page she has marked, she maneuvers the volume through to me, scrutinizing Stout. "Pretty bold to haunt a priest," she says, and I'm sure she's speaking to Marvin.

"Wait," Butterfield chimes in, "he's haunted?"

"Not a priest," Mama corrects. "He's Methodist minister."

Daddy finishes. The circle complete, Sam uses his ability to float the crystals into the four directions around it.

"How are you doing that?" Butterfield screeches.

Tabby sits and I swear she smiles. Persephone nods at me. "Go ahead."

"Marvin Goodwin," I say, recalling Winter's instructions, "you are not welcome here. Remove your spirit from the body of Reverend Stout."

"Not likely," he crows through Stout's lips. "I'll have my revenge!"

Butterfield presses his body as far away as he can get, up against the bars. "Get me out of here! This violates my rights!"

"Shut up," Mama and Logan say in unison.

"You should make your peace with what happened, Marvin." Reasoning with vengeful spirits rarely works, but I feel the need to give them a chance to redeem themselves. "It's time for you to move on."

Stout's head swivels to me, his eyes nearly black. "I'm having too much fun."

Where's Sherlock and his rational logic when I need it? "This man did not harm you, and it's bad karma to take your failure out on him."

"I never failed!"

Not too surprising he sees it that way. Many live with the idea that their misfortune is someone else's fault. At times it actually is. "But you made the decision to turn bitter and wish ill on another. You tried to kill Smith Stout, and what happened? You ended up harming yourself." I think of Patience and the poison, of all the atrocities committed out of hurt and pride. "Not the best use of your time and energy."

He jerks on the bars and when they touch the iron, he flinches. "You can't hold me here forever."

"Actually, the circle will contain your ghost as long as it's intact, and technically, I only need another minute or so to remove you by force from the reverend's body." I raise the book, flashing him the spell. "Trust me, I've done this before." I don't mention the part about the previous spirit getting loose, or the fact I died and Logan had to resuscitate me. "I have no qualms about doing it again. Your choice."

"I'll find a way to break free and come for you," he spits.

Logan moves beside me, lending his support and protection. "You can try."

I grin and Logan winks at me. "Last chance," I say. "Exit on your own or I'll force you out."

"Witch," he seethes. "Try it."

I glance at Butterfield, frozen in shock. "Just to clarify, I am not a witch," I tell him. "I'm just a medium."

"I'm a witch," Sage offers, raising her hand.

"What?" Butterfield half-whispers.

"For your fictional character," I remind him. "You wanted to know what it's like to deal with spirits? To get under my skin so you can make your ghost-whisperer jump off the page? This is it."

His jaws move, along with his lips, but no sound comes out.

I begin the spell. "Evil spirit be laid to rest. Release your hold and return the host. Energy spent for evil and bane, go back now from whence you came."

Stout's body shakes, the cuffs clink against the iron bars as Marvin desperately attempts to hold on. His features contort. "You...can't...do...this."

"Into the circle I send you this hour." I raise my voice to be heard over his cursing. "May any attempt to harm turn sour. So mote it be!"

"So mote it be," Sage intones.

Marvin's essence begins to lift out of Stout, his ghostly clutches no longer strong enough to maintain the bind. A keening rings through the jail, causing me to drop the book and all of us to cover our ears.

As Stout's knees go weak, I gesture at Logan. The two of us catch his near-limp body and keep it from crashing down into the salt circle. Marvin's spirit is ejected and trembles as it glares at me. "You witch!"

"What... What happened?" Stout asks, looking from me to Logan.

"Undo the restraints," I tell Daddy.

A *click-click* and they're off. Logan hauls the minister over the salt line without disturbing it, and Mama helps guide him to the seat.

Tabby makes her way to me, as does Persephone, the three of us standing along the edge of the circle, taking up the points where the crystals hover. Sage moves into place on her side of the bars and a sudden surge of energy sweeps around us.

Marvin, less cocky and raging, dashes around his new prison. "What are you doing?"

"You need to cross over," I state. "It's time."

He races to me, but the boundary stops him. He bangs against the invisible wall. "I won't go!"

Butterfield pipes up. "What's happening? Is there a ghost in that circle?"

This time all of us tell him to shut up.

Reverend Stout finds his voice. "I don't understand."

Sherlock appears. "Ah, sorry I'm late."

"You're *always* late," Persephone growls.

"Hello to you, too, dear," he replies and gives her a smile that makes her blush.

There's another ghost with him, one I recognize. Just like the last time I saw him, he's wearing a white shirt, black pants, and has a large gold cross around his neck. "Brother Dupree?"

"Ava, you are doing the Lord's work, and I have come to assist you."

Before when the infamous, knock-em-down Methodist preacher intervened, things went south in a hurry. He's the reason my ghost escaped the salt circle at Christmas and sent her black magick into me. "I think we have it covered."

He floats across the barrier and greets Marvin. "Where have you been, Brother Goodwin? Your congregation is waiting for you."

"Who are you?" Marvin stops his gyrating and frowns. "What congregation?"

"Yours. They've missed you." Dupree motions to some far off place where this imaginary—or perhaps it's real—group exists. "I've been filling in for you, but I'm no Marvin Goodwin. We preachers have to stick together, right? But I can't fill your shoes. They've been praying for you to come home."

Marvin shifts back, wary. "You're lying."

"Never!" Dupree is a showman and looks aghast, grabbing at his chest as if the dig hurts. "I have never, and will never, lead you astray."

After a moment, Marvin's expression softens, his shoulders slump. "I can't, even if I wanted to. I've done something...bad."

Everyone who can't see the ghosts watches me and Sage.

"What are they saying?" Butterfield asks no one in particular. We ignore him.

Dupree makes a dismissive sound in his throat. "You paid for your sin and all is forgiven. The good you did, the folks you helped? That's your legacy."

"My flock turned on me." Marvin's voice is dejected. "I gave them everything and that's how they repaid me."

"They were human." Dupree gives him a patient smile. "Our Lord said, 'forgive them for they know not what they do.' They are no longer bound by the ego, as you shouldn't be either. It's time to forgive and take them back into your fold. That is what we do. We hold ourselves to a higher standard, like the Good Lord Himself. We forgive those who trespass against us."

Marvin seems to think this over. It's torture to stay quiet and let it sink in. Finally, he gives a tiny nod. "Jesus would want that."

"He does," the other preacher assures him.

"I don't feel well," Reverend Stout says.

Mama shushes him and pats his hand. "You will in a few minutes."

"You must mean a lot to them," I say to Marvin, trying to reassure him. "They're counting on you."

Marvin faces away. "I mean nothing to them."

I glance at Sherlock. He gives me a *be patient* gesture.

"Now, now, that's not true." Dupree places a hand on Marvin's shoulder. "They're hungry for your message, as well as your forgiveness. You are wasting your time on this plane. We've got a holy-rollin' revival going, and I need you to lead it."

"Smith Stout is there." Marvin's voice is bitter, and it's almost a question. "Let him take care of it."

"Smith is the most worried about you, brother. He holds no grudge and wishes only for the two of you to join forces in the afterlife."

Marvin sniffs but seems intrigued. "He does?"

Gotcha.

Sherlock catches my eye and winks.

"You bet he does. He's not above reproach, the way he slunk in and stole your flock. He seeks your forgiveness, too."

Marvin grows taller. He nods as if he agrees. "Of course he does."

Dupree smiles wide and holds out a hand. "Shall we go talk to him? See your congregation? They will welcome you with open arms."

Slowly, Marvin extends his to meet it. "I would like that."

Instantly, a white light appears in the corner of my eye. "Go to the light," I tell him. "Brother Dupree will accompany you."

He glances at me, then Stout. "He'll be alright?"

I nod. "I'll take care of him."

"Break the salt line," Sage instructs as Dupree puts his arm around Marvin's shoulders.

I hesitate, hoping Marvin won't trick us and end up back in Stout or one of us. I pick up the kyanite blades and hand them to Logan, Mama, Daddy, and Stout. "Hold these."

If Marvin tries to enter me or Sage, he'll be flat out of luck. The cross is in my pocket and Sage wears an amulet to keep herself protected. Bis will have to take his chances.

"What about me?" Butterfield cries. "Why aren't you giving one to me?"

"Autograph those books or I'll shove one down your—"

"Ava," Mama scolds. "Manners."

Swallowing the rest of my words, I use a toe to scrap away some salt.

Quick as lightning, the ghosts fly toward the glowing light. Right before they disappear, Dupree looks back at me and tips an invisible hat in my direction. "Keep up the good work, Ava!"

"They're gone," I tell the others when they disappear. Mama and Logan pelt me with questions, and I answer as best as I can.

Daddy unlocks the cell, Butterfield watching me intently, as I explain what happened. We clean up, and Logan helps Stout stand.

The reverend hands me back the kyanite. "I believe I may have said some things I now regret."

"Keep it," I tell him in regards to the crystal. "And take this, too." I give him the cross. "For now, keep both on you at all times, okay?"

"I best be going." He heads for the open door.

I follow, picking up his Bible and handing it to him. "We really do want you to participate in the ceremony tomorrow night."

Mama lays a hand on his arm as we walk him to the station exit. "It would mean so much to me and Nash. I won't take no for an answer."

"I would like that, Miss Dixie," he says, offering her a shaky smile. "Hard to believe it's been thirty years."

She pats his back. "Ava will be in touch with the details."

He turns to me. "Thank you," he says, and then he's gone.

24

I get up at five to work on Mama's dress. Fueled with coffee and sugar, I pin the hem on both layers. Rhys sees my light on, awake early himself to fix breakfast for the B&B guests, and comes over bearing cranberry orange popovers.

He pulls a face when he sees me at the sewing machine. "What are you doing?"

The heavenly scent makes my stomach growl. "Mama plans to wear her plain blue suit today. Daddy wants her to have something more elegant. I didn't have time to hire Gloria to create a whole new dress, so I'm modifying one that belonged to Queenie. It can be Mama's something borrowed."

He shoos me from the chair and starts adjusting the pins. "Sugar, why didn't you say something? I'll whip this out in no time. Do you have your script laid out?"

Not really. I unfold the napkin covering the food and pick out a fat popover. "I'm putting the final touches on it right now. In my head," I add when he raises his brows.

Pins between his teeth, he makes the shooing motion again. "Go write it down."

"You're my hero." I take the delicious treat with me and head for the attic. There's something I need to check.

Thank goodness Aunt Willa never threw much away. As I down the last bite, and stumble over a couple of old chairs, I see a fancy box from a dry cleaners, long out of business, sitting on top of a dresser.

The single bulb hanging from the apex of the open ceiling doesn't illuminate this area enough, and I didn't think to bring a flashlight. I wrestle a wooden three-legged table out of the path after stubbing my toes and grab the box.

It's coated with dust, and heavy. I lift the lid to see a white garment bag inside. This must be it.

Carrying the whole thing downstairs, I sneeze a couple times, my nose itching, but manage to wrangle it into the spare room.

The sewing machine hums under Rhys' skilled fingers. "Thought you were working on your speech."

"I needed to check for this first. I think it's Mama's original wedding gown. Aunt Willa wore it, too."

Placing the lid aside, I draw out the garment bag. Rhys stops to watch and gets up to help me with the layers of lace and tulle. "My, my, that is something," he says, examining it. "Straight out of the sixties."

It's not quite the way I remembered from the video of the wedding. It seemed more glamorous and beautiful, probably because Mama was wearing it. Her bigger-than-life personality gave it something the gown lacks without her in it.

Still, it makes me smile. "I have an idea," I tell Rhys. I inspect the back where a giant bow rests at the top of the skirt. It's gaudy and limp after years of being pressed flat, but the satin is white and shiny. As I suspected, it has a loop to hold the train. Hidden snaps allow it to be removed.

"Your Mama is in great shape, but she can't wear that anymore." Rhys points to the neck and lacy skirt. "And I'm not sure she'd want to."

I chuckle. "She wouldn't be caught dead in it. Didn't much

like it the first time, according to what she said last night. All I need is a piece of it, though, for a souvenir."

Releasing the material of the bow, I go to work pressing the wrinkles from it before I cut out a small handkerchief. This dress was a beauty in its day, and even though not her style, it holds dear memories. Mama should have a memento of it to carry as well.

"Can you do embroidery on this?" I ask Rhys.

He's finishing the top hem. "Sure can," he tells me. "Why?"

"Excellent. Show me how."

❧

Rosie arrives at eight to prep for Jenn and Jeremy's wedding. The morning air is humid but the sky clear, and the birds chirp a cheerful song.

Logan and Brax get the dozen chairs lined up near the gazebo and we decorate them with white bows.

Betty arrives with the flowers, some in buckets, and others with vials of water on them to keep them fresh. All Jenn could afford was a small bouquet, so I supplemented from my own funds, as a wedding gift to her. Betty assists Rosie and me as we embellish the chair bows with miniature roses and baby's breath. Then we add lights and more flowers to the gazebo.

"I have an interested party who would like to rent your building," I tell the florist. Although already familiar with the layout, Rhys is chomping at the bit to do an official walk-through and sign the agreement.

"You?" she asks with a hopeful smile.

"No, Rhys and Brax," I clarify. "They have to move the Thorny Toad, and your place would be a good fit for them."

"How lovely. Well, they better hurry. I've already had interest in it. A buyer for the building, in fact."

Rosie staples a bow to the podium. "Who?"

"A gal from out of town. I don't know her, but she plans to open a bakery."

My heart falls. "Has she made an offer?"

Betty picks up an empty bucket previously filled with cut flowers and dumps out the water. "Marla says she might today."

Carrying a stack of buckets, I walk her to her van, reviewing our setup for the anniversary party as we go. "See you at two," she says, pulling away.

Or a bit sooner. I wave her off, and then bop over to the B&B, texting Marla as I dash up the steps. Inside, I locate Brax and Rhys, who are chatting with two guests in the parlor.

"Do you need help with the affair?" Brax asks.

I shake my head. "We need to go see the florist shop now," I tell "Someone from out of town is after it."

"What?" Rhys nearly comes out of his skin. "But it's ours."

Brax hustles him from the parlor and we convene in the foyer. "Who told you this?" Brax asks, his voice low.

My phone vibrates with an incoming text from Marla. "Betty. She was just here to help set up for Jenn's ceremony." I read the message. "Marla will meet you there in twenty minutes. Go."

Rhys grabs my arm. "You have to come with us."

"You don't need me."

"Please," Brax says with a depth of emotion in his eyes that always gets to me. "It will make Rhys feel better if you're there."

I check the time. "The wedding is at ten-thirty, and I have more prep to do."

"We'll help you with whatever you need," Brax insists. "As soon as we convince Betty to rent the place to us."

"I can't leave Rosie on her own."

"She won't be." Rhys points out the transom window. Penn is parking out front. She exits the car with a garment bag in one hand, and a tote in the other. She's brought her dress for the ceremony, and the bags of bird seed I put her in charge of making.

He grabs his keys from the hook near the door and takes Brax's hand. "Please, Ava?"

I can't let them down. I text Logan, telling him what we're doing and the fact I'll be back shortly. He sends back a thumbs up emoji. "Okay," I say to my friends. "Mission: Convince Betty is underway."

25

The offer from the other party comes in while we're doing the walk-through. Marla gives Betty the details in the kitchen, as Brax, Rhys, and I stand outside and discuss what to do.

Betty doesn't immediately accept, telling Marla she wishes to sleep on it. She knows Brax and Rhys, and that gives them an advantage.

I'm back at The Wedding Chapel in plenty of time for Jenn. I finally get to meet her groom, and although Jeremy is more reserved than our bride, he's just as excited. The grin on his face goes from ear to ear, and soon, we're off and running.

Jenn glows as she comes down the short makeshift aisle, the eyes of her family and closest friends watching. The couple have chosen two songs and a poem, and they've written their own vows. Simple and beautiful.

I realize I never got to hear Daddy's song for Mama. Guess it will be as new to me as it is her, and that's just fine.

During the ceremony, I notice Tabby lying on the back porch steps, her sleek body in the sun. Sam hovers close to her, both watching as I pronounce Jeremy and Jenn husband and wife.

Logan arrives after having an errand to run, and presides over the official document signing. The weather holds, the group gathered celebrates, and we throw bird seed when the time comes and our happy couple takes off for their brief honeymoon.

"Another one in the books," I say to Willa when I'm upstairs gathering Mama's dress.

"Brother Dupree is right," I hear my aunt respond. "You're doing good work here, Ava. I'm so proud of you."

"I hope you can make it to the vow ceremony," I say.

"Look in my jewelry box, will you?" I don't usually see my aunt, only hear her, but I notice a tiny wisp of white from the corner of my eye. Making my way to the standing chest that holds a lovely collection of both good and costume pieces, I open it up. "See that bracelet with the sapphires?" I nod and pull it out. "Take that to your mother for me." Then her voice grows faint as she leaves. "She'll know what it means."

Logan is downstairs waiting—and so are my grandparents.

"Your betrothed is a lawyer?" Samuel glowers at me. "I shall not have it."

The original town laws set up by him and Tabitha were simple—no rum, no slaves, and no lawyers. "Sorry, gramps, you have no say in this," I inform him, "and Logan is a good man, regardless of his vocation."

The man in question eyeballs the room. "Who are you talking to? It's Sam, isn't it?"

I move to the door, Tabby slipping into the front window display. "He's upset about you being an attorney. Just ignore him."

We join Rosie and Penn in the van and head for the Nottingham Hotel. Penn thanks me over and over again for giving her sister a beautiful celebration.

The next few hours fly by as I coordinate with the hotel owners, Baldwin and Kalina, to prepare the ballroom, dining area, and outdoor space for the vow renewal and reception. They've done the prep work and are happy to help with more.

Queenie brings the food and takes over the kitchen. Even Sage and Bis make an appearance and offer their help.

When Reverend Stout and his wife show, he looks much more himself. They, too, dive in and lend a hand.

Mama and Daddy arrive at three. I take Mama to the bridal suite, Daddy claiming he wants to practice his vows. "I have a little surprise for you," I tell her, and lead her to the gown hanging on the full-length mirror.

She gasps and covers her mouth with a hand. "Oh, Ava, it's beautiful. Did you design it?"

"Queenie and Rhys get all the credit, but this…" I give her the handkerchief with the original wedding date, as well as today's, embroidered on it in her favorite shade of blue. "Is all me."

Holding it tenderly, she reads the numbers and her eyes tear up.

"It's made from the original dress. This one"—I touch the gown hanging on the mirror—"is something borrowed from your best friend. Something old, something new, something borrowed and something blue—we have all the bases covered."

She throws her arms around me and gives me a hug that squeezes the air from my lungs. "You are amazing."

"Don't cry or you'll ruin your makeup." I break the embrace and grab my purse. "Aunt Willa instructed me to give you this from her jewelry collection."

"You still have that big ol' chest?" Mama asks, accepting the bracelet.

"Of course." I may tell ghosts it's time to move on, but I can't quite let go of my aunt or her things. "She said you would know what it meant."

Mama places it on her wrist and I assist with the clasp. "I haven't seen this in years." She slides it around. "This was our mother's."

"Grandma Edwina?"

Mama nods. Edwina died when I was in high school. I

remember the reunions with her side of the family that she would drag us to every summer upstate. With her gone, no one gets together like they used to.

"It's perfect," I say. "Are any of your extended family coming today?"

There's a touch of sadness in her eyes. "A few sent congratulations, but they're all busy. You know how it is."

Queenie knocks and peeks in. "Is it time to get dressed?"

We welcome her in with her garment bag, and she heads for the washroom to change.

"I'm going to need some AV equipment," Mama tells me.

A last minute surprise. My favorite. "We've already set up the microphone and the photographer is videotaping the ceremony. What else do you need?"

"You'll see. I asked Baldwin to arrange two big screen TVs on the lawn. Don't be alarmed when you see them."

Wondering what she has up her sleeve, I kiss her cheek and leave the two of them. Downstairs, I see the televisions flanking the trellis, wound with ivy and jasmine, and Baldwin connecting them to speakers. Logan is helping.

"Any clue why Mama wants this?" I ask the men.

They shake their heads.

"Can I steal you away?" I shield my eyes from the sun, and watch Logan as he finishes connecting his cord to a laptop on a table nearby. "I need to practice my part of the ceremony. Will you be my audience?"

He grins. "Anywhere, anytime."

At four on the dot, we're all in place and a sea of chairs stretches over the lawn. I cue the music, as the sun shines over the lake in the distance. Reverend Stout was agreeable to my idea and walks Mama down the aisle between the onlookers, while Daddy waits under the trellis with me.

Mama looks stunning, and Daddy is rocking a suit with a pair of his favorite motorcycle boots. Queenie walks behind Mama, a simple flower in her hair. Landon Jones stands in as Daddy's best man.

Logan is in the front row, smiling proudly. I can't wait until he and I are the ones committing to each other.

Once Stout hands Mama over to Daddy, the minister joins me in front of them. He leads us in prayer and welcomes all in attendance.

I gaze over the people I know and love, my eyes snagging on Helen and LC, seated in the last row. It's rare indeed for Logan Charles Cross, the second, to leave the winery at all, but I'm relieved they've shown up. Chuck is nowhere in sight, and I wonder if he's cancelled his plans to visit.

The ceremony goes off without a hitch. Daddy has his guitar nearby and sings his vows to my mother, making her cry. Good thing she has the handkerchief—it's not all that absorbent, but still comes in handy. At the ready, I sneak a tissue to her when it's her turn.

She has created a video, splicing photos and short recordings of our family together and has it set to music—the original song they danced to at their reception. As that plays on the screens, Mama takes the microphone and speaks over it. "The first time I met you," she says when a photo of a high school football game appears. It's old and grainy. "I knew that night that you were my soulmate."

"Aww," some of the crowd say.

"I vow to continue honoring your strength because you are mine."

Daddy smiles, and his eyes look damp, too.

The next few photos walk us through their dating years, college, then we arrive at their wedding. A portion of the recording I watched hundreds of times plays on screen. "Just as we vowed that day," she tells him, "I will be by your side always. I will support you in sickness and health, for richer and for poorer, but let's put the dying part off for a long, long time, shall we?"

Daddy grabs and kisses her, bending her backwards. She

drops the microphone as the video rolls on. I see a picture of me as a baby, and then a few more of the three of us as I grow up. I finally reach over and tug gently on Daddy's suit jacket. "Save it for later, kids."

Those in the nearest seats laugh and the two of them break apart. Mama wipes at her messed up lipstick and then does the same to Daddy's lips.

The video continues on as I take their entwined hands and raise them. I nod at Stout and he places his on theirs as well. "We now pronounce you, once again," we say in unison, "husband and wife."

A cheer goes up from the crowd and clapping ensues.

After the photographer snaps a few pictures, I stick them in the atrium to receive well-wishes from those attending. Queenie changes out of her dress and starts on the dinner preparations. The DJ kicks on the music in the ballroom, and folks begin to stroll around, talking and laughing.

"I can't believe your parents showed," I murmur to Logan.

He's helping me take down the trellis while Baldwin disconnects the TVs and sound system.

In a Sensei voice, he asks, "You doubt my power, grasshopper?"

"Never," I tell him, smiling. "If it weren't for your mother, I'd make you marry me here and now."

He grabs me by the arm and pulls me in close. "What's she got to do with it?"

The depth of love I see in his blue eyes makes me feel a touch lightheaded. "Oh, just everything."

"Say the word and I'll hire the good reverend right now."

"Be careful or I will. We don't have a marriage license, though, and your mother would kill us."

He shrugs. "Minor details."

We laugh and I know I'm the luckiest woman alive. "Did Chuck bail on dinner?"

"Nope. Mother already left to go home and get things cooked."

I finger his lapel. He's wearing one of my favorite suits. "Do you think he's getting married? Is it a secret baby? Did he win the lottery?"

Logan seems to consider all of those possibilities. "He doesn't even have a girlfriend, so I doubt it's marriage. Secret baby, maybe. Guess if he shows up in an Aston Martin, we'll know it's the lottery."

"I'll be waiting with bated breath for you to text and tell me what it is."

He strokes my shoulder. "You'll know when I do because you'll be there with me."

"Oh no." I back out of his arms and shake my head. "Helen will have a stroke if I show up."

He doesn't let go, hanging on to my arm. "She will not, and you're going to be part of our family, so they'll all have to get used to having you around."

I mentally groan. I'd planned to enjoy tonight, dancing, and gorging on Queenie's delicious catering. Attending a stuffy dinner at the Cross household is not fun.

I smile anyway. I will go to the ends of the earth for this man, and that includes putting up with his family's idiosyncrasies. "Alrighty then," I say through clenched teeth. "I can hardly wait."

❦ 2 6 ❦

Knowing I'm going to eat light later, I make sure to get plenty of Queenie's appetizers in my stomach. As I'm buzzing around the tables loaded with a few of my favorites, I bump into Candace.

"My mother is no tech wizard," I say, grabbing a mini crab quiche to add to my growing pile. "Did you help her with that video montage?"

She scoops cut up fruit from a bowl. "It was no big deal."

"Well, thank you anyway. I appreciate it." I add a couple of the skinny parmesan breadsticks. Logan likes those. "How's married life?"

"What?" She gives me a confused glance as we move down the line.

I point to my ring finger where my diamond shines. "You and Austin?"

"Oh, right." She glances toward the next set of bowls and platters. "It happened so fast."

"You haven't dated long?"

A woman farther down spills ambrosia salad onto the buffet table and the line stops moving. "We've known each other for a while through the dinner group."

"What did you think of Amos Butterfield? Louise mentioned he was trying to give you script pointers that night."

Queenie and Winona Redfern rush from the kitchen to clean up the mess. Winona runs the thrift shop but moonlights when Queenie has a big catering job.

Folks begin snaking around that section of the table, but more are determined to wait for a fresh bowl of the delicious treat. Candace makes a face. "He was annoying."

"You didn't like his suggestions?"

"I think he was more interested in getting me alone in the library."

I pop a grape into my mouth, sensing his motives went beyond script discussions. "Did he act inappropriately?"

Her gaze flicks to Buster and Baylor at a table with Louise between them. "He was drunk. I went in there to practice my lines, and I guess he followed. He took the script from me and started marking things out and writing new stuff in. I mean, it was a mystery dinner with small-town actors. We're not exactly Golden Globe material."

I don't correct her that it's The Tony Awards for theatre. I get her drift. Winona arrives with a new bowl. "I didn't think Louise served alcohol at those functions," I mention.

Candace shrugs as the line begins to move again. "He must have had some before he came."

Buster and Louise laugh loudly over something Baylor says. "Sure is a relief that Louise is okay," I say, helping myself to a spoonful of pistachio pudding. "Good to see them all getting along."

Candace bites into a cucumber slice stuffed with cream cheese. "Sure is, especially after what I—"

She catches herself and looks away.

"After what, Candace?"

Her gaze flicks to the threesome again. She motions me to follow her away from the line and lowers her voice. "When Butterfield and I were in the library between the shelves, Louise and Buster came in. He was…kissing her, and she was laughing. I wanted to sneak out the other door—I didn't want them to know I'd seen them—but I was afraid they would, anyway, and Butterfield wouldn't give me my script back."

"Buster's been sweet on her for a while."

"Oh, I know, but he told her he didn't want to keep their relationship a secret anymore. That he loved her and wanted everyone to know. She got upset and insisted he not breathe a word of it because Baylor would freak."

"I can't believe Baylor didn't already know. Seems a lot of people did."

"Buster stood firm about not breathing a word of it to her, and left Louise crying next to the display case. I thought I could sneak out at that point, but Butterfield kept making shushing motions and whispered about this being great fodder for one of his books. Louise texted someone and then just sat there, worrying over her ruined eye makeup. I was dying for her to leave so I could get back to the dinner. I knew Austin was looking for me."

Queenie rolls a cart by, filled with deserts and candies to another buffet table Katrina and Baldwin are setting up, and we move out of the way. "Eat up," she urges. "There's plenty more."

"It's all delicious," I tell her and she beams. I turn back to Candace. "Did you get your script back?"

"I did, but with Louise in there, I was still stuck. Butterfield was nearly giddy, making notes on his playbill. I thought Louise was about to finally leave when Baylor came storming in and went off on her."

"Baylor? She wasn't at the dinner."

"I think that's who Louise texted. She must have decided if it was so important to Buster, she'd confess to his sister about them. Baylor was livid and said she wouldn't stand for it, and that Louise was no good for him. I thought they were going to get into a knock-down, drag-out cat fight." She glances around.

"Butterfield loved it. He told me that was real motivation for murder, right there."

I press my lips together for a moment, considering his rudeness. "What happened?"

She plays with another slice of cucumber. "I got out of there, that's what. I didn't want to see or hear any more of that soap opera, and I had to get away from him. He kept touching my arm and acting like he was fixing my outfit." She gives a visible shudder. "Gross old man."

I digest this, no longer as excited about my food. "You think Baylor stabbed her?"

Her eyes slide left then right. "After Detective Jones found Louise? Butterfield said it had to be Baylor. He also said Louise would never tell. He's right, too. They're best friends now."

We both glance at their table. "Why wouldn't Louise come clean if she knew Baylor attacked her?"

Candace frowns at me as if I'm dense. "Because she'd lose Buster. Can you imagine accusing your lover's sister of trying to kill you? That wouldn't go over well, especially if she ended up in prison because of it. Buster would hate Louise forever if that happened."

I see her point, but something doesn't add up. I'm sure Baylor didn't arrive at the Society until well after I did. Did she flee after the deed, then return to comfort her brother? "You told Detective Jones all this?"

"Most of it. I left out the bit about Butterfield getting handsy. I didn't want Austin to find out."

When she stares pointedly at me, I assure her I won't say anything. "My lips are sealed, but you shouldn't feel the need to keep it a secret."

"Are you kidding? Austin would kill the guy, seriously, and then I'd end up with *that* on my conscious."

Not to mention having her newly betrothed with a prison sentence to fulfill. "Jones must not feel there was enough evidence to charge Baylor."

"He didn't believe me." She lifts her chin in defiance. "I could see it in his eyes. He acted like I made it up."

Our detective often behaves that way. It's part of his demeanor, never letting on what he does and doesn't believe and/or know.

"You'd think he'd be on the war path to figure it out and put whoever it is behind bars," she continues, her focus now on Jones, who is chatting with a group outside the atrium doors.

"Why do you say that?"

Another of her *duh* looks spears me. "Because he's in love with Louise. He had to be upset about her and Buster, and maybe *he's* the one who did it."

The echo of Butterfield's words. "You really think Jones is capable of such a thing? That he has *murder in his heart?*"

Her face screws up at the use of those words. "It was obviously an act of passion."

Which didn't answer the question. "He's a strong guy. The knife surely would have gone in farther."

"Maybe he realized what he was doing and what the consequences would be."

"Hmm. Maybe."

Logan finds me and touches my elbow. His eyes are lit up like it's Christmas. "Did you see the dessert table?"

"Talk to you later," I say to Candace and let him lead me to it.

Once there, I encourage him to indulge. "I need to speak to Detective Jones. I'll be right back."

He checks his watch. "We better leave in ten."

I set down my plate and nod, but he's already selecting a triple-chocolate brownie and eyeing his favorite candies.

"Can I speak to you for a moment?" I ask Jones.

He begs off from the group and follows me to a giant palm surrounded by blooming lilies. "Nice event. Your parents seem happy."

"Thanks. Glad you could make it." I move behind the plants

to make sure Candace doesn't notice me, and ask him about her story. "Did you follow up on what she said?"

He gives me an indignant look. "Why can't you leave the detective work to me and just enjoy the celebration?"

"I am enjoying it, and I'm a concerned citizen who may have learned more about that night at the mansion. I wanted to share information with you."

He sighs with resignation. He knows how stubborn I am, and probably figures indulging me is simpler than fending me off. "Did you smell alcohol on Butterfield that night?"

"I never got that close to him."

"Not one person saw Baylor at the Society until she arrived after seven. I asked Louise about the text and she claims she sent it to Buster, saying she was sorry, that he was right and they should come clean."

"You believe her? Did you ask to see it?"

He sets his jaw, as if searching for patience. "You think I don't know how to do my job?"

"You're the best detective around." I try not to choke on the words. Mama always says you catch more flies with honey, and I'm prepared to lay it on thick if necessary. "I'm simply trying to understand why Candace would make this up if it's not true."

"You don't need to worry about the case, and yes, I saw the text. I have everything under control."

"I don't doubt that for one minute."

"Mr. Butterfield was quite upset when I arrived at the jail this morning. Said you were doing voodoo stuff in there last night."

I give him an innocent face. "That man has a very active imagination."

He rolls his bottom lip in and then huffs. "Candace is trying to throw suspicion on Butterfield about the whiskey in order to take the spotlight off Austin."

I already figured that, and I couldn't care less about the bottle of liquor. "This whole elaborate lie over Louise, Baylor, and Buster is to cover for her new husband?"

He shrugs. "The things we do for love."

She doesn't seem like a woman in love to me. "Has Butterfield confirmed or denied this story?"

"Outside of his complaints about you, he hasn't said a word since asking for his lawyer."

That in itself is suspicious to me. "You're holding him on a separate charge. Why won't he comment about Candace's story, if he had no part in what went down?"

Jones just stares at me, unyielding.

This serves to convince me there is more going on, and our good detective believes so as well. "If not Baylor, who do you suspect?"

His face is stony. "Keep your nose out of it, Fantome, or I'll sic your father on you, y'hear?"

As he strolls away, Logan joins me, handing me a brownie wrapped in a napkin. "Energy for the road," he says, and we move to leave.

$$\text{❧} \quad 27 \quad \text{❧}$$

On the way to Cross Winery, I stew about Candace's confession.

If that's what it was.

Logan listens, but I can tell his mind is on the upcoming dinner.

"Jones could be right," I admit. "She might simply have made up this whole story, attempting to cover up Austin's theft."

"Mmm hmm."

I chew a pinched off piece of brownie, the chocolate melting on my tongue. "Butterfield could clear the whole thing up if he'd answer a few questions. So why won't he?"

Logan takes the highway heading north to the hills. Night is coming, the last rays of the setting sun peeking through the trees and blanketing the farms. "Thought his lawyer was arriving today."

"Yes, but that may not help. Even if he did catch Candace in the library to rewrite the script, he may not admit to it since she's accusing him of being drunk and acting improperly toward her."

"What happened to the script and the playbill? Those might be evidence to confirm Candace's story."

"Good question." I text Jones, asking about both, and finish my treat. I don't expect a reply, but it's worth pursuing. "Do you think our detective has a crush on Louise?"

Logan makes a face. "Landon? No, why?"

"I think he likes her, and may have taken her attempts to recruit him to join the Society as flirting. Butterfield suggested he may have stabbed her after finding out about her and Buster. Said he'd made it look as if Buster did it, and he found Louise in the nick of time and rescued her to manipulate her feelings for him."

Laughter fills the car. "No wonder he writes fiction."

That makes me feel slightly better. "Butterfield's pointing a finger at Jones; Candace at Baylor. We know Jones was there when it happened, but no one can confirm Baylor was."

"Doesn't mean she wasn't."

We pass a pair of horses walking toward a barn. Their owner waves at us, and we return it. "But someone would have seen her. There were two dozen people in that place."

"And most were in the dining room, waiting for the mystery theater to begin."

"True, but as Butterfield says, I don't think she has *murder in her heart*." I make air quotes. "Even if she were raging mad at Louise, could Baylor stab her in the back?"

"In a moment of emotional overload, sure. When she did it, reality struck and she didn't drive it all the way in, was horrified, and ran off."

"And again, no one saw her."

"Except maybe Butterfield and Louise."

"Louise is sticking to her story about not seeing the culprit, either because it's true or she's protecting someone."

He takes the turn to the vineyard. "She would protect Buster, which might mean lying about Baylor, but she wouldn't Landon."

I ball up the napkin and check that I don't have chocolate on my lips. "Is there anyone else she might protect?"

"Austin, I suppose."

I face him. "Austin?"

Logan shrugs. "They're not close, but he *is* kin."

My jaw drops. "They're related?"

"He's her nephew." He angles into the drive. "I thought you knew."

Small towns. Everyone's related. "His aunt is stabbed and he leaves town to get married?" I shake my head, a whole new scenario unrolling in my mind. "He was stealing the whiskey, probably with help from Candace, and Louise caught them. He attacked her, but had a change of heart. Candace is covering for both of them, making up the story about her and Butterfield."

Jones replies, reminding me he has everything under control. *I'm sure you do*, I type out, *but it's Austin*, and then I list the facts pointing to him.

What comes back makes me seethe a bit. Jones sends me a winky face.

I show Logan the screen as he parks outside the Cross mansion. "What is this supposed to mean?"

He exits the car and comes around to open my door. "It means he already knows. Come on. We have a dinner to get through, and since there's no Aston Martin out here, it doesn't look like Chuck won the lottery. Scratch that one off our list."

❧

THE MOMENT I MEET TRYSTA, "WITH A Y, NOT AN I", SHE tells us when Chuck introduces her, I feel nauseous. She doesn't offer a hand, and I'm relieved, since I fear touching her might send me to the bathroom, heaving.

Her aura is cold, roiling. I'm not overly sensitive to other people's energy in general, but there's something very wrong with hers.

Chuck is his usual boisterous self, pulling Logan in for a manly hug, and offering me one as well. I'm not the huggy type, but I make the effort, and allow a quick, emotionless embrace.

While Logan is fair like his mother, Chuck resembles his dad, with darker hair and a lankier build. He talks nonstop, as LC pours glasses of red wine, and we make small talk in the formal living room.

"I saw her," Chuck says, hand around Trysta's waist, "and I knew I was done for."

So much for not having a girlfriend. They smile into each other's eye, and her energy coils like a snake around him. "He's my white knight," she states, breathy. "I'd be destitute without him, my dreams in tatters."

I take a step back, pretending to be interested in the fabric on the sofa. Logan accepts the glasses from his father and hands one to me. "We're so happy for you."

I lift mine and pretend to sip. The brownie is not sitting well, and I don't want to cause a scene.

"You're here." Helen whisks into the room, apron on, and not a hair out of place. Even the pearls around her neck gleam, no sign in sight that she's actually been in the kitchen since leaving the party.

She smiles at Logan before turning to me. "You look pale, Ava. Are you well?"

Normally, I'd take that as one of her digs, but I'm really *not* up to par. I suck it up and return her fake smile. "A long day, is all. I'm delighted to be here."

Her smirk, there and gone in a heartbeat, tells me she knows I'm lying.

There's no engagement ring or wedding band on Trysta's finger, so I rule out secret marriage or baby. When it's time to eat, we take our places at the table, and I manage to get down some soup and fresh baked bread during the first course.

Chuck regales us about his and Trysta's first meeting at the Kroger, both going for the last packet of yeast on the shelf. "She knew her yeast, that's for sure," he says, "and it was love at first sight."

"I had no idea he ran the brewery," she elaborates, "but any guy who can talk yeast is the man for me."

He flushes slightly, and Trysta leans against his arm. "She's a baker," he tells us, mooning at her. "She's too sweet for words."

My stomach tightens.

She giggles and pinches his side. "You goof ball."

Helen arrives with the main course—roast beef and potatoes—putting an end to their flirtation. Everyone digs in, complimenting Helen, and LC asks Trysta what she likes to bake.

I mostly move my food around, listening as the conversation flows. I can't place why Trysta's energy affects me so, but I'm exhausted and cranky by the end of this course, barely able to sit still.

"I found the cutest place," she says. "And it's right here in town."

"Not yet," Chuck murmurs.

She bats her eyes at him and jiggles in her seat. "Please? I'm so excited. We have to tell them!"

"You're buying Betty's place?" I ask, even though I already know.

She nods. "That's the one. Chuck and I are moving in together, and I'm opening a new bakery! Can you believe it?"

Persephone appears behind her, grimacing. "This one's trouble." She glances at me and there's fear in her eyes. It makes my skin crawl.

Suddenly, as if she's lifting a curtain, the angel waves an arm. Three male ghosts appear, all with significant cords attached to Trysta's back.

I jump up, nearly knocking over my chair. All eyes turn to me, including those of the ghosts. "I'm sorry, I need to, uh... Excuse me."

Legs trembling, I rush from the dining room and down the hall to the expansive powder room. Inside, I splash water on my face and towel it dry. "Who is she," I whisper to Persephone, "and why is she attaching herself to Chuck?"

"More like, *what* is she?" The angel appears to sit on a chair in the corner. "She's a type of ghost, but still has an enormous amount of energy and is able to appear human."

"She's got three battery chargers, that's how."

"That's part of it, but she needs a human to anchor it, like a grounding wire."

"And Chuck is it."

She nods.

Before we can discuss it further, Logan knocks on the door. "Ava? You okay?"

I yank my phone out and text Rhys. "Fine. I'll be done in a minute, but I'm going to beg off early, okay? I need to get home."

He peeks his head in and sees me texting. "Is this about Louise and the stabbing? Or the fact my brother's fiancée is buying the florist shop out from under your friends?"

"They're your friends, too," I remind him. "And...wait, fiancée?"

He nods. "Chuck just proposed."

❦ 28 ❧

I tell Logan Brax can pick me up, planning for us to stop at Betty's and convince her not to sell to Trysta. Logan nixes the idea and insists he'll take me home.

Helen seems relieved I'm leaving, yet miffed that Logan is, too. We say our goodbyes, and I feel ten times better when we get out of the house and away from Trysta.

I explain what I saw to Logan on the drive, hating every minute of it.

"That's nuts," he says, and then chuckles without humor. "Chuck always did know how to pick 'em."

"Persephone thinks she's a ghost, but not like any I'm familiar with." I lay my head on the headrest and close my eyes. "To tell you the truth, I'm rather sick of all of them."

He reaches over and pats my knee. "Any idea how we can unhook this one from my brother? Is he in danger?"

By the look of the three connected to Trysta, it's possible, but I don't want to worry him needlessly. "I have to check into it because I honestly have no idea. At the moment, I'd say she needs him alive and healthy."

"Outside of being sickeningly in love, he seemed okay."

I agree. Unfortunately, being in love with her could cause things to get ugly.

My phone vibrates with a text from Brax. "Swing by Betty's," I tell Logan. "Brax and Rhys are meeting us there. We have to put a stop to this sale." For two reasons, now.

We hit the city limits and I swear, I feel better with every passing mile we put between us and Trysta. "They'll just go somewhere else," Logan states.

As long as it's far away from me and mine, I'm okay with that. But Chuck is Logan's brother, and my soon to be brother-in-law. "When are they getting married?"

"No set date yet, but I have a feeling it will be soon. The good thing is, Mother doesn't like her, so maybe she'll talk sense into him and break them up."

Never imagined I'd want Helen to have such power, but right now, I'm cheering hard for her.

We pull into Betty's a few minutes later. Brax and Rhys are on the porch with her. Each is in a rocking chair and Rhys is explaining his plans for offering outdoor seating.

Betty is smiling and nodding, and gives Logan and I a little wave. "Don't worry," she tells me. "I've already agreed to rent to these boys. You know I have to give weight to my hometown neighbors."

I'm literally so relieved, I sag down right on the top step. I'd prepared to beg, borrow, and steal this place to keep Trysta from getting her hands on it. "Thank you." I feel my tension draining fast, and an almost giddiness replacing it. "I can't tell you what a good decision that is."

She makes a slight face. "There's something about that baker gal I couldn't quite put my finger on, but it made me feel weird."

Like you want to throw up? I want to ask her, but I don't.

"Sorry, Logan," she says to him. He's watching me, his foot on the bottom stair. "I know your brother is fond of her. Don't understand why they want to move here, with his business being in Marshall and all."

"We just found out about it," he tells her, not taking his eyes off me. "I'm not certain myself."

"Ava, are you okay?" Brax asks.

Weariness after the day's events is zapping my strength again. "I need sleep. It's been a crazy week."

"Would y'all like to come in for a nightcap?" Betty offers.

"I better get Ava home." Logan reaches for my arm to help me stand.

Brax and Rhys rise to go as well. Rhys takes Betty's hand and bends over it. "Thank you, Miss Betty. I can't tell you how much this means to us. I promise, we'll pay extra each month so we can own it in no time."

She pats him. "I expect free food and a reading once in a while."

We all laugh. "You got it," Brax tells her.

We say our goodnights and leave. Once we're back home, us heading to The Wedding Chapel, and them to their B&B, Rhys stops us. "What was that all about?"

"We do not want Chuck and Trysta to set up that bakery in our town," I tell him and Brax. "She's bad news."

Once more, I explain what I witnessed and pass on Persephone's beliefs about her being a ghost. Both look stunned.

"It's never dull around here," Rhys says, "but it seems like things are more squirrelly than usual, doesn't it?"

I couldn't agree more.

Logan offers to come in and make me a cup of tea or draw me a bath. I ask for a raincheck. My only plan is to hit the sack and not get up until noon. Sunday, blessed Sunday, means I have twenty-four hours to recoup. I've done all I can for the moment to help Samuel, Reverend Stout, Brax, Rhys, and Detective Jones. Jenn's ceremony, as well as Mama and Daddy's, was a success. I can finally collapse.

He kisses me at the door and I watch, as usual, as he crosses to his side of the street. "I'll bring brunch tomorrow, once you're up and moving around."

I wave. "I love you!"

He calls the sentiment back to me.

"Gag me," the knocker says.

Inside, the house is dark and quiet. After hanging my purse on the hook near the door, I kick off my shoes and yawn. Leaving the lights off as I head for the stairs, I don't even worry with my phone. My plans are simple—strip down and fall into my nice, soft bed, ignoring the world for the rest of the night.

A silhouette emerges from the shadows in the hall, making me stumble back. The features are obscured but the form is familiar. "Good work turning the police on that kid," the man says.

My insides go cold. "What are you doing here? I thought you were still in jail."

Amos Butterfield follows me as I take several steps back the way I came, a slash of moonlight cutting across his face and showing me his calculating grin. "My attorney handily got me out, just like he always does, and sequestered any official reports or details that might be leaked to the press."

I swallow the lump in my throat, a wave of revulsion gripping me. "Like he always does?"

"The true art of writing murder is to understand your character. You're well aware of how I get into that frame of mind."

"You attacked Louise."

He watches me like a predator assessing its prey, him advancing as I retreat. "Would have killed her, too, if your cop friend hadn't interrupted me."

Heart racing, I calculate how fast I'll have to be to get to my purse, my phone, the door. "But why? You don't even know her."

"She had the right circumstances surrounding her and a cornucopia of potential suspects."

"And Austin is so easy to manipulate." Candace comes up behind me. "He was the perfect fall guy."

I whirl toward her, then motion at Butterfield. "You... You're helping *him*?"

She ambles over to a gown still on the rack and fiddles with it. "We were supposed to meet up in Mississippi and then go on to Dallas together. He's going to help me become the writer I've always dreamed of."

"But then you had to mess it all up," Butterfield growls, "getting me arrested for assault."

I ignore him and focus on Candace. "How could you do this to Louise?"

"Are you kidding? She's a loser like the rest of you. I'm getting out of this town and I won't look back."

"Why haven't the two of you left already?"

"One last plot thread to wrap up." Butterfield stalks toward me, flashing one of my knives. He uses it to point to the kitchen. "We want to make sure Austin is framed and no one ever looks into the situation further."

Through the open doorway, a dark shape lies unmoving on the floor. "Persephone," I say under my breath. "Could use some angel mojo now."

"That was quite a performance at the jail last night," Butterfield comments. "You almost had me believing you're the real deal."

"It's all to get attention," Candace assures him. "She's got half the town convinced she sees ghosts."

I don't have time or energy to worry about whether they believe me or not. If Austin's in there, he must be injured or dead.

Which means, I'm next.

"Persephone," I say louder. "Tabitha, Samuel, Sherlock? Anybody?"

None answer.

"Just in case, I did throw salt in a circle around the house," the author explains. "Keeps the ghosts out, too, doesn't it?"

Bugger. "You got me," I lie, raising my hands as though I'm surrendering. Technically, neither Tabby, nor Persephone, are ghosts. They can cross that obstacle without issue. "It was all a pretense, sort of like you using your alias as a writer to kill people."

"I've never murdered anyone."

The fact he says it with a straight face, while holding a knife and threatening me, is confounding. My attention flicks between him and Candace. He's blocking my way upstairs; she's doing the same with the route to the front door. That leaves the kitchen. "So you instruct other folks on how to do it?"

Pride lifts his lips. "I've studied the intricacies of killers in great depth. It's what makes my stories come alive."

That confirms my worst fear—if he's admitting to having a hand in this charade, he's planning to kill me as well.

Or, I guess, have Candace do it. I glance at her. "You haven't committed murder yet. He's some kind of weird serial killer; don't let him get his jollies from watching you do it. He's using you, Candace. How many other desperate writers has he lured into this game? Where are they now? You don't mean anything to him. You're simply a means to an end."

"You're wrong." She fists her hands. "They're famous, just like he is. I want to be, too."

She must be desperate to believe that lie. "This isn't the way to do that."

"Austin is so drunk, he won't remember killing you, but his prints are on everything," she tells me. "He'll be going away for a long time."

Persephone pops in. "She's too far gone to reason with."

I'm relieved that at least I have some backup. "About time you showed."

She glances toward the front window. Sherlock hovers on the porch. "Blame him."

"Is the salt keeping him out?"

"Yes."

I swear under my breath.

Candace and Butterfield become uneasy, eyes following mine

to the spot I'm talking to. Then Butterfield chuckles. "Nice ploy, but your ruse won't work this time, Ms. Fantome."

"Tell me something only he knows," I beg the angel.

"Seven," she says. "He's tricked wanna-be writers into killing seven people in order to *understand their characters*."

Sick to my stomach, I face the mad man. "Seven. That's how many innocent people you've made others kill for you. That's one for each book in your series, isn't it?"

His face blanches. "That's a lucky guess."

"Give me something else," I demand, "and then get Logan."

Persephone floats to the kitchen doorframe, staring in at the still unmoving body on the floor. "Four of them were young, gullible women like Candace, two were older. He preys on females, because they tend to be more desperate and easier to trick, and by the way, Logan went back to his parents' house."

My two attackers can't hear her, of course, but a bit of their doubt seems to slip away as I continue to carry on the conversation. "He *what*? Why did he do that?"

"Because he's worried about his brother."

Can't blame him, but he needs me to stop Trysta, *if* that's even possible. "What is he thinking?"

Butterfield, not sure if I'm talking about him or Logan eyes me warily, shifting the weapon between his hands. "You really are unbalanced, aren't you?"

"There's the pot calling the kettle black." I repeat what Persephone has told me about him to Candace. "You want to write a mystery novel? Here's your chance to solve a crime, rather than commit one. Pen a nonfiction story. It'll be a *Lifetime* movie, I guarantee it."

Persephone gives me a nod. "It has potential."

Before I can reply, she disappears. "Great." I toss my hands up. "Even my guardian angel has deserted me."

"I'll be right back," I hear her say, even though I can't see her. "Have a little faith."

"Can we get on with this?" Candace asks Butterfield.

He holds out the knife. "Use this. Remember what we discussed, into the belly, but angled up toward the heart."

As she moves to take it, I see my chance. I'm out of time, and there's only me to save myself.

With all the gumption I can muster, I jump her and take her to the floor.

She's scrappy, but I outweigh her, thanks in part to Queenie's three pound brownie. We hit the ground hard and I grab her ponytail and yank.

A cry of surprise fills the room as her head snaps to the side. Butterfield, chicken that he is, shuffles back as we pencil roll over and over each other, both striving to get the upper hand.

"Kill her," Candace shouts.

"You must do it," the author counters.

The knife lands beside us, clanging on the wood.

Candace and I both look at it, our breathing ragged. We have to release each other to reach it, and I can see her deliberate over the odds, just like I'm doing.

Decision made, I give her a shove and clamor for the weapon.

From the corner of my eye, I see Tabby sneak into the room. Next comes Sam and Sherlock. The salt line must be broken. The ghosts cheer as I grab the handle, the males shouting instructions.

So focused on the knife, I barely notice Butterfield lifting the paperweight from Rosie's desk. As I bring the blade around to slice Candace's arm, he chucks the heavy ball at my head.

Lucky for me, Candace lunges at me, putting herself in the line of fire. The paperweight slams into her right temple, then ricochets and smacks me in the throat.

She topples, howling with cry of dismay mixed with pain. I shriek, too, but my larnyx constricts and I can't make a sound.

"Get up!" Sherlock shouts.

"Watch out!" Sam bellows.

"For crying out loud," Butterfield yells, "can't you do anything right?"

Candace falls face-first to the floor and doesn't move.

Rising, I seize the knife and pivot to stab the author in the leg. "Shut up," I croak, driving it in deep.

He howls and suddenly, Bis bursts through the kitchen door. He jumps over Austin and slides to a stop a few feet away. "Ava, I'm here!"

Butterfield stumbles back, jerking the weapon from his leg. He glances at Candace, still unconscious, and runs out the front door, trailing blood after him.

Bis helps me gain my feet. "Samuel said you were in danger. I got here as fast as I could. What happened? Are you okay?"

I glance at my great-grandfather. "Thank you," I whisper, rubbing my throat.

Sam nods. "You are most welcome. I salute your bravery. Your courage reminds me of your grandmother's."

Tabby meows from her front window seat. Arthur and Lancelot appear on the stairs, yawning and curious about the commotion.

Sherlock stares out the open door. "Don't worry, our felon didn't get far. Detective Jones has already apprehended him."

"I called him on the way," Bis tells me. "He said he was in route."

Persephone appears. "I made Logan turn around." She points to Candace. "What should we do with her?"

Tabby hops down and stalks to the woman. She raises a paw, claws out, and reaches for Candace's face.

"Don't," I command, although a part of me would like to see my grandmother extract some justice. My voice is still not working right and I sound like a croaking frog. "Leave her to Jones."

A few minutes later, the detective muscles his way in after Bis and I have Austin sitting up. The missing bottle of whiskey is half empty next to the poor kid, and his head lolls to one side as we endeavor to wake him. "Ambulance is on the way," Jones tells us.

I'm not sure if Austin's truly drunk as a skunk, though he does smell like a brewery, or if he's been hit in the head. "Good, he needs it."

"It's for you," Jones corrects.

"I'm fine," I insist, rubbing my injured throat.

"Sure you are." He lifts me by an arm and scoots me out of the way. "Get out of here and let me do my job."

Sirens float on the distant night air. Brax and Rhys come running in as I sink into a kitchen chair.

One look at me and they both pale. Logan arrives and Bis brings me a dishtowel with ice in it and I hold it to my throat. I explain what transpired in as few words as possible, but the effort still strains my injured windpipe.

When the ambulance arrives, Reverend Stout, in his white dress shirt and black pants, clears Aunt Willa's office of everyone but Logan and me so he can examine my wounds. His partner goes to Candace.

Logan hugs me tightly, then holds my hand as Stout checks me out. Jones leaves to take Butterfield to the station, but not before telling me I'll need to give my official statement come morning. He's placed Candace under arrest, too, but she needs medical attention and will be in the hospital under concussion watch.

"Butterfinger's lawyer won't be able to get him out on this one," Logan assures me.

All I want to do is crawl in bed and sleep. Stout insists I let Doc see me. Logan takes me to the clinic and explains what happened when Mama and Daddy arrive.

After tests show my trachea is bruised, Doc prescribes rest and no talking. Persephone teases me about it all the way home, her and Sherlock riding in the back of Logan's Porsche.

I may not have murder in my heart, but my imagination comes up with plenty of things I'd like to do to Candace in retaliation.

Logan and Mox stay the night and I sleep until noon the next day. I'm pleasantly surprised to find I have a voice again. It's weak, but after some hot tea and a shower, I feel almost normal.

Once Logan is assured I'm okay, he leaves to take Moxley for a walk and prep his cases for the coming week, promising to be back later. On the porch, I check in with everyone, getting updates on Austin, Candace, and Butterfield. Brax and Rhys bring me lunch, and show me some of the ideas they have for transforming Betty's place into theirs.

Mama and Daddy stop over as well, wanting the full scoop. My voice is wavering, so I beg off going into details and send them away as soon as I can to enjoy their second honeymoon. I text Winter to let her know how things turned out, and that I'll call later in the week when my voice is up to a full blown conversation.

The phone rings with others checking on me, but I let them go to voicemail. They'll all understand when I tell them it was doctor's orders.

Baylor, Buster, and Louise stop by with flowers. Louise hugs me and tells me she's grateful I cleared Austin from any wrong doing, and uncovered Candace's treachery. Buster shakes my hand, also appreciative that I've removed suspicion from Baylor.

As those two leave, Baylor lingers a moment. "What should I do with all those books that jerk signed for us? Burn them?"

I shake my head. "Are you kidding?" I half-whisper. "They'll be worth even more now. We're selling them and donating the funds to the families who lost loved ones because of him."

She hugs me. "Brilliant. I'll get on that tomorrow."

Back on the porch, I'm enjoying another cup of tea, antici-pating Logan's return. He claims he's fixing dinner tonight, and I wonder what that might involve.

As I contemplate that, a ghostly form catches my eye down by the homestead. It's Samuel.

Tabby has been AWOL since Logan brought me home from the clinic, even forgoing food when I put kibble in the cat dishes. I assume she's there, too.

Taking a fresh cup of tea with me, I amble down there, what to do with Samuel on my mind.

I find them talking and laughing in the kitchen, Tabby in human form without a stitch of clothing on. "Sorry to interrupt," I say.

There's one of my robes on the wooden chair and she wraps it around her. "Ye not be crossing him over. Not yet."

I sit. "He has to choose to go on his own. I can't force anyone."

Her chin rises all the same. "We need time."

He reaches out and takes her hand. "I'm not leaving you."

The look they share makes me glance away, feeling as though I'm intruding on a private moment. "The thing you felt drawn to in this house," I ask Sam. "Did you figure out what it is? Is it the symbol on the fireplace?"

He shakes his head and points "It was her. She's always been my anchor."

My great-grandmother blushes. "And you mine, husband."

I toy with my mug, a sense of well-being washing through me. "I was hoping you'd stay for my wedding," I tell Samuel. "It's not until October."

He straightens, a smile causing the skin around his eyes to crinkle. "I would be honored, Avalon."

Tabitha smiles, too. "Our last descendent happy. This is our dream." She glances at me. "How many children do ye plan to birth, love?"

"Let's not rush things," I croak. "I'm not even sure I can handle marriage."

Another glance passes between them. "From what I have witnessed," Samuel says, "you shall do just fine."

❧

THAT NIGHT ON THE SOFA, BELLY FULL OF LEFTOVERS FROM the reception—Queenie helped Logan with his dinner preparation—and heart happy, I let Logan massage my feet. Two glasses of the Cross winery's finest chardonnay sit on the coffee table. Moxley and the cats, excluding Tabby, are lying on the various pieces of furniture.

It's too warm for a fire, but Logan has soft music playing, and we're discussing all the changes that are coming, between Brax and Rhys' move, our wedding, and the situation with Chuck and Trysta.

"She was pretty upset about Betty not selling that property to her," he tells me. He had lunch with his parents, along with Chuck and Trysta, who are still in town. "Are you sure about her being a ghost? I didn't feel anything weird last night or today when I was around her."

I'm too blissed out to let the memory of her energy upset me. "I'm sure."

"I reckon we need to keep an eye on them, keep her close, if you're to figure out what and who she is and stop whatever she's planning with Charlie, right?"

I squirm a bit, wishing we could postpone this conversation, but he's worried and I need to reassure him as much as I can. I reach for my wine and take a swig. "Might be challenging since they're going to be two towns over."

"That's the thing. They want to live here, now." He stops massaging and stares at the dark fireplace. "She's convinced Chuck to move back to Thornhollow and commute to his brewery every day. Regardless of the deal with Betty falling through, they're going to remain here."

I shift my feet to the floor and sit up, rubbing my head. "That will at least make it easier to watch her and uncover what her plans are."

"Exactly." He stands and walks to the fireplace, leaning on it. "That's why I've decided to rent my building to them for the bakery. They can live above it in my apartment."

"You did what?"

Persephone materializes. "It's a good idea." She plops into the rocking chair. "Looks like we're dealing with a black widow."

Logan doesn't realize she's there, and I'm staring at him dumbfounded. "Hear me out. They'll be right across the street. We can keep an eye on them."

"What about *your* business?"

He gives me a hopeful smile. "I'm going to rent that empty room you have."

Currently, I store miscellaneous wedding supplies in there. "You're moving in?"

He takes the glass from me and sits on the table, setting it down. His hands encompass mine. "We're getting married June first."

My jaw drops. "I can't get everything ready that fast. Your mother will kill us."

He strokes a lock of my hair behind my ear. "You've always dreamed of getting married in June, right?"

"Yes, but..."

"We'll do a small wedding in the backyard. Nothing fancy, and then we'll have the big blow out my mother wants this fall."

"We'll get married twice?"

"Why not?" He kisses me, then rests his forehead against mine. "I'd do it a hundred times, if it makes you happy."

"Isn't that sweet?" Persephone chimes in.

"I don't know what to say," I tell him, but the idea is appealing. I'll get what I want and Helen will, too. Win-win.

He squeezes my hand. "Say yes."

"Do it," Persephone urges.

Tabby, in cat form, strolls in. Samuel floats in with her. "That sounds most agreeable," he states.

My head spins. I laugh. "I would love that. Do you think your mother will go along with it, though?"

He shrugs. "It's our wedding. I want her to be happy, but we have final say in how we do this."

The vision of a small, intimate wedding in the backyard makes me nearly giddy. "Okay then."

Persephone and Samuel clap. Tabby seems to nod at me before leading Sam away.

Moxley raises his head, sensing something has happened, but then flops back down. My cats crack open their eyes, yawn, and return to sleep.

"You two have fun," Persephone tells me as she rises from the chair. "Tomorrow, we get to work on that black widow."

She disappears, thankfully, and I smile at the man in front of me. "I can't believe we're doing this."

"You never fail to amaze me," he says.

"Back atcha." I wrap my arms around his neck. "I'm the direct descendent of Samuel Thornton and Tabitha Holloway, and it's time for me to step up and act like it. This is my town, and I'm going to protect and nurture it with everything I've got."

"I think you've already done a pretty good job."

I kiss him. "You haven't seen anything yet."

STAY TUNED FOR MORE ADVENTURES WITH AVA, TABBY, Logan, and the rest! ***Corpses and Cupcakes* coming early 2022!**

Have you read the Sister Witches of Raven Falls Mystery Series?

Click here to get your copy of *Of Potions and Portents* so you can keep the magick going!

And be sure to sign up for my reader newsletter so you're the first to know about new releases, giveaways, and other cool stuff (including pet pics, crafts, and recipes)!

YES, I want Nyx's Cozy Clues Newsletter!

BONUS, YOU'LL RECEIVE A *FREE BOOK* FROM THE SISTERS OF Raven Falls Series that includes cute magickal spells, recipes, and craft ideas!

Don't miss the next exciting adventure! Sign up for Nyx's Cozy Clues Mystery Newsletter.

And check out these magical stories!

Sister Witches Of Raven Falls Mystery Series

Of Potions and Portents
Of Curses and Charms
Of Stars and Spells
Of Spirits and Superstition

Confessions of a Closet Medium Cozy Mystery Series
Pumpkins & Poltergeists
Magic & Mistletoe
Hearts & Haunts
Vows & Vengeance (August 2021)

Once Upon a Witch Cozy Mystery Series
If the Cursed Shoe Fits (Cinder)
Beastly Book of Spells (Belle)

Poisoned Apple Potion (Snow) - only available in the Black Cat Crossing box set which is FREE when you sign up for the Whiskered Mysteries newsletter!
Red Hot Wolfie (Ruby)
Hexed Hair Day (Rapunzel) 2021

ABOUT THE AUTHOR

USA Today Bestselling Author Nyx Halliwell is a writer from the South who grew up on TV shows like Buffy the Vampire Slayer and Charmed. She loves writing magical stories as much as she loves baking and crafting. She believes cats really can talk, but don't tell her three rescue puppies that.

She enjoys binge-watching mystery shows with her hubby and reading all types of stories involving magic and animals.

Connect with Nyx today and see pictures of her pets, be the first to know about new books and sales, and find out when Godfrey, the talking cat, has a new blog post! Receive a FREE copy of the Whitethorne Book of Spells and Recipes by signing up for her newsletter http://eepurl.com/gwKHB9

CONNECT WITH NYX TODAY!

Website: nyxhalliwell.com

Email: nyxhalliwellauthor@gmail.com
Bookbub https://www.bookbub.com/profile/nyx-halliwell
Amazon amazon.com/author/nyxhalliwell
Facebook: https://www.facebook.com/NyxHalliwellAuthor/

Sign up for Nyx's Cozy Clues Mystery Newsletter and be the FIRST to learn about new releases, sales, behind-the-scenes trivia about the book characters, pictures of Nyx's pets, and links to insightful and often hilarious *From the Cauldron With Godfrey blog*!

I hope you enjoyed this story! If you did, and would be so kind, would you leave a review on Goodreads and your favorite book retailer? I would REALLY appreciate it!

A review lets hundreds, if not thousands, of potential readers know what you enjoyed about the book, and helps them make wise buying choices. It's the best word-of-mouth around.

The review doesn't have to be anything long! Pretend you're telling a friend about the story. Pick out one or more characters, scenes, or dialogue that made you smile, laugh, or warmed your heart, and tell them about it. Just a few sentences is perfect!

And if you're interested in crystals, psychic readings, energy healing, astrology, or past lives, please visit https://crystalswithmisty.com/ to find out more about how these all-natural, fun services can help you live a calmer, healthier life!

Blessed be,

Nyx 🤍

ACKNOWLEDGMENTS

Thank you to Erika Melrose for suggesting the bloody knife in the time capsule! It was the perfect addition to the story.

Thank you also to my resources for the info on skeletons, magick, and police procedures. While I take some liberties to make the story more interesting, I couldn't do without the input of experts!

Finally, thank you to the fans of Ava and her family. I LOVE getting your messages and emails about how much you enjoy the characters, including Tabby and the other animal companions. Initially, I only planned to write three books in this series. Now, because it brings me so much joy, and you all seem to enjoy the series too, I've decided to keep it going as long as you, the readers, want.

Blessings!
Nyx